NO WEAPON

AUDREY MCKAY

Two Shoes Publishing House

No Weapon

Copyright © 2010 by Audrey McKay

This is a work of fiction produced from the author's imagination. Any similarities to living persons or actual events are coincidental.

ISBN 978-0-9842933-4-6

Cover art: modified from Original by Gary Hathaway © – License purchased at dreamstime.com

EXCERPT

Sidney sighed. "I simply wanted you to know where I was coming from. So when I say things that may not seem to make any sense at the moment, give me a little lee-way, OK?"

Past experience had taught him well and he knew better than to agree to something so vague. "Things like what?"

"Like, what if I told you I know you didn't just randomly show up at the health expo or walk up to me tonight. You were sent to protect me."

He sat motionless, had even stopped breathing at some point. No one had ever picked up on his cover before. Not once. It was one of the things he prided himself on. If he needed to be a drug dealer or a diplomat or a charming ladies man, he became that person. He had a natural ability to blend into every possible demographic. So how did this one woman with no background in espionage pick up on him so easily? His senses went on high alert and he felt like he had just been busted in a sting.

Clearing his throat brought no relief from the things he was feeling so he grabbed his glass and took a long swallow. When he was sure he could speak in a normal tone he set the glass back on the table. "Why would you say something like that?"

"God told me."

"What else did He tell you?"

She gave a furtive grin. "Nothing else about you so you can relax."

DEDICATION

This book is dedicated to my heavenly Father, His Son Jesus Christ and the Holy Spirit. I would not have been able to do this without them. I also want to dedicate this book to a very special friend of mine by the name of Darling Richards who experienced an unimaginable loss while I was writing this book. Even in her grief she managed to encourage me to keep writing and words can't express how appreciative I am. Finally this is dedicated to everyone who has figured out that it's possible to find joy on the other side of pain.

No weapon formed against you shall prosper, and every tongue that rises up against you in judgment you shall condemn. This is the heritage of the servants of the LORD, and their righteousness is from ME says the Lord.

(Isaiah 54:17)

Half the harm that is done in this world is due to people who want to feel important. They don't mean to do harm... (But) they are absorbed in the endless struggle to think well of themselves ~ T.S. Eliot

Prologue

"You've done a good work here Canaan."

Pastor Canaan Styles looked around the large edifice once more before opening his office door and stepping aside. "Thank you Bishop. Come on in and I'll get you something to drink before we have to go into the service. We have a while before the praise team finishes and the deacon gets up to say the prayer."

Bishop Montgomery entered the office and sat down in one of the cushioned chairs opposite a Large LCD screen. "Yes, that was quite a tour. You've accomplished so much and at such a young age. Your father would have been very proud."

"Thank you, sir." Canaan handed a full glass to the older man. "And here's your pineapple juice, with a slice of lemon just the way you like it."

Bishop Montgomery took the glass and slid back in the large padded chair. "Thank you my boy. Next we'll look forward to those sons of yours carrying the vision forward." He beamed at his young protégé. "You've started a great legacy to move into the next millennium."

Pastor Styles smiled as he grabbed a remote off the table and sat down next to the Bishop. "We can watch the service from here so we know when to go into the sanctuary."

Bishop Montgomery grinned with genuine pride. "Yes sir, Charles sure would have been proud of you."

Canaan smiled broadly once again before turning the large screen on. They watched as the cameras panned back and forth over the choir and the congregation. The large choir clad in long red robes swayed to and fro wooing the crowd through one slow selection then whipping them into a frenzy during the next. This went on for several minutes before Bishop Montgomery leaned forward in his seat. "Who is that young woman in the purple dress Canaan?"

Canaan barely looked at the screen. He knew whom the elder man was referring to before the question was past his mustached lips. "Ahh, I'm not sure Bishop. Which young woman? There are so many."

The older man stood and walked closer to the substantial flat screen. He kept his hand near the TV so that he would be ready to point when the camera fixed on her again. "There! Right there, see her on the left side of the sanctuary about the fourth row back."

He tried to keep his disdain in check but he saw her all right. Every Sunday for the last three years, he saw her. Sidney Lyons, the bane of his existence. Never the less he put on a suitable smile before he answered. "Oh yes, that's Sister Lyons."

The old man drew his face closer to the monitor. "She is..."

Canaan sighed. "She's beautiful, I know."

"No." The older man shook his head. "It's more than that. She's very attractive, yes, but there's something else there. The glory of God is all over her, like I've never seen it before. Well, actually I saw it once before on a young man from the south when I was doing a revival there last year. He was about her age and just like him then, the anointing of God is literally pouring out of her."

"So I've heard."

The bishop spun around with wide eyes. "You don't see it?"

Canaan doubted the older man was seeing anything but a pretty face and a nice figure but he wouldn't dare put a voice to that thought. He couldn't understand why so many renowned men of God kept saying the same thing about this...girl.

'She's anointed, she's blessed, she has the glory of God all over her.' As far as Canaan was concerned, Sidney Lyons was nothing special. She was more suited to be under the submission of some man than to manage the things of God. Everyone knew that was better left to men. Besides, he was almost certain that she was still with that rock star, that coffee, latté, java fellow, whatever his name was. But he had been through this before and he knew if he didn't agree quickly the other man would waste valuable time trying to convince him of her virtue. To appease the old man and get the conversation moving he offered up what he could. "Yes, I suppose there is something there."

Bishop Montgomery looked at his young charge a second longer than was comfortable. "Of course there is something there." The dim eyes grew bright with excitement. "God must be up to a new thing! He has something very big planned for her Canaan. I see a prophet's mantle on her. She's going to need the best training. She will stand before kings and queens. Make sure you help her along the way. The enemy will try to stop what she has to do but I can see the hand of God on her. Son, you make sure you support her. She is going to need all that she can get."

Support her! Canaan was incensed. He had spent the better part of his life building the church they were standing in. He had sacrificed countless hours with his family to pour into the congregation here. He himself had just recently gotten to the point where his members would offer to support him without asking. What would he look like helping some girl get to a high-ranking level in ministry without her putting in any work for it? Besides, he reasoned, Bishop had been chastised in his younger days for preaching that the top tiers of the five-fold ministry could belong to either a man or a woman.

Everyone knew that women couldn't get past the rank of teacher. If that ever happened it would potentially put them over men. Everyone knew that women, especially the more feminine ones were relegated to roles of teachers and some churches didn't even let them teach men. All pastors, prophets and apostles were supposed to be men. Everyone knew that. No sir! If God had planned for her to be a teacher then she would have to get there the same way he had, through hard work, sweat and tears. *I am the pastor of this church and I don't give support, I receive it!* He steeled himself to remain calm as he answered and nodded graciously. "Yes Bishop, certainly I will. We should probably head in to the sanctuary now."

Bishop Montgomery tore his eyes away from the TV only for a second. "Yes, of course." He murmured one more "remarkable" before he actually turned away.

Once in the sanctuary the two men took their places in the pulpit and stood with everyone else as rapturous music filled the air. The song was an old hymn and had been a well-known staple with every established denomination for at least the last century. It took Canaan back to a time when he was a boy and his father Charles was the pastor of this church. He recalled one Sunday in particular when as a youth of just five or six he was expected to recite long passages of scripture in front of the whole church. He had almost gotten through the whole eighth chapter of the book of Jeremiah without making any mistakes when he stumbled on the phrase 'balm in Gilead'. He said 'gom in billy dad'. Everyone laughed at what was a cute and almost expected mistake by a small child but Canaan paid dearly for his mistake when he and his family finally arrived home late that evening. After being made to recite the passage until it was perfect, he received forty lashes on his tiny bare body with a wet leather belt.

His dyslexia wouldn't be discovered until his teenage years and when it was, he was brought before the elders for deliverance from the 'demon of dyslexia' in a private service. The session lasted all night and into the next morning. When testing the next week revealed that he hadn't been relieved of his affliction, Pastor Charles Styles tried to drown the devil out of him. Canaan's dear sweet mother had saved his life that night by threatening to call the police on her husband. She of course paid dearly for that threat, as she knew she would, but she reasoned that she had saved her son's life with those words. That was the last noble deed she would accomplish before taking her own life the next day.

When Charles arrived home to find his wife dead he sat down and took a moment to gather his thoughts, then he read the small, crinkled piece of paper in her hand. It simply said *'I can't take another day of you'*. The suicide note Mary Styles left her husband never saw the light of day. It was burned in the fireplace before the authorities were called to remove the body from the home, along with any other evidence of spousal abuse. Of course questions arose when a state medical examiner noted the fresh bruises as well as the number of bones that had healed over time. Though as a member of the prominent church, the young medical examiner made sure that any questions concerning the right reverend were answered to everyone's satisfaction and as rumors often do, they eventually faded away.

Canaan moved out a few days later knowing what his father was capable of ...and recognizing that the only buffer he had ever known was now gone forever. He was pulled back into the present just as the choir was ending the hymn. The harmonious voices of the choir and the congregation rose and fell in unison as they softly crooned the words *All to Jesus I surrender. All to Him I freely give. I will ever love and trust Him, in His presence daily live...*

The future belongs to those who believe in the beauty of their dreams ~ Eleanor Roosevelt

CHAPTER 1

Several months earlier...

The beautiful bells rang out for everyone to hear. The cheering crowd and bright lights were almost too much to take. She spun and dipped and wove her way through every obstacle until she saw she only had a few hundred yards to go. She broke the ribbon and crossed the finish line with an easy stride. During her victory lap she descended down through the clouds and the warm breeze, past the birds and the trees until she landed softly in the thick grass. It wasn't until then that she woke up.

Wiped Out. Sidney barely moved as the sun peeked through the dark wooden slats on the window. She was awake but she couldn't move. Her niece and nephew who had just turned one-year old last month had taken her for a ride yesterday. Her oldest niece Kyra had come along to help and Sidney smiled knowing that Ky was the only reason she had made it through the day. Jenna, the baby girl had started walking early and was into, under and on top of everything she could reach. Her brother Leo hadn't started walking yet but she knew it was only a matter of days. He sat on the floor literally drooling after his sisters as they walked by him.

Sidney smiled once again as she thought of all the giggles and tears she experienced in one day. She loved the dynamic duo as she had taken to calling them but they were more than a handful. She wondered how single parents do it, especially with more than one child. Those babies were constantly on the move and if Jenna, who was a tiny version of her brother-in-law by the face, went one way, it was almost assured that Leo, who was the spitting image of his mother, was headed in the other direction unless it was time to eat. Even though he couldn't walk yet he was a faster crawler than Jenna was a walker. Kyra sensing her aunts' lack of baby handling skills managed to help keep them corralled to the living area when they were inside. Several hours at the park yesterday afternoon had worn them all out and when her sister Sidra and brother-in-law came to pick them up last night, everyone was asleep. Jensen rang the doorbell three times before Sidney stirred.

"Girl, I was about ready to kick the door down." Jensen stood in the doorway and looked down at Sidney as she rubbed her eyes.

"Man your kids wore me out. I had no idea. Come on in."

Her sister Sidra was right behind him and hugged her as she came in. "Trust me, I know what you're saying."

Jensen headed over to the three lifeless bodies sprawled out between the sofa and the T.V. and started gathering their things together. He looked up at Sidney with a teasing glint in his eyes. "You know, we could leave them here and pick them up after church tomorrow."

Sidra laughed at the look on her sister's face. "Jensen we need to keep her around for at least 10 more years. Don't scare her away."

"Yeah, I guess you're right." He had just strapped Jenna into the pink and brown covered car seat sitting against the wall and was reaching for Leo when Kyra's eyes fluttered. "Come on big girl, time to get home."

Kyra mumbled something unintelligible and turned away from them. She was out like a light two seconds later. Sidra just shook her head and reached for one of the now heavy car seats. Jensen just shrugged his shoulders as he looked down at his oldest daughter. "That girl will take 30 minutes to wake up if you give them to her."

Sidra had just reached the door and turned around to smile at her husband. "I wonder where she got that from."

He smiled back at his wife with the other car seat in hand. "I have no idea what you're talking about." They both laughed on their way out the door. Jensen turned to Sidney before he crossed the threshold. "I'll be back for her in a sec." Sidney nodded as she looked over at the tall nine-year old stretched out on her floor. She had grown so much over the last few years. It was obvious to everyone that she had inherited her father's height. Some people were already guessing her age as 12. *Jensen better get his shotgun ready.* Sidney knew it was only a matter of time before little boys would be beating down the door to get to Kyra. She laughed inwardly when she imagined what Jensen's reaction would be to those little boys. *Poor things.* Jensen came back and scooped Ky up in a flash. When they left she checked the doors and security system and headed for the comfortable bed waiting for her upstairs.

After slapping the snooze button for the third time, Sidney decided to sit up in bed. She was already going to be late for church at the rate she moving. She had started going to Hearts Desire Ministries a few years ago, shortly after her suicide attempt. She had been in such a bad space then. She'd found out at the age of thirty-five that her father wasn't dead like she had been led to believe since birth and that she had a brother and sister around her age to boot. The celebrity she had been dating decided to spaz out on her that very weekend and even tried to get violent. Of course she defended herself but it was her word against the super star and he had super money to back him up.

When the sister she had only known for a day agreed to represent her in court she thought she had hit the jackpot. They ended up becoming very close until one night when Sidney made one very bad decision. She kissed her sister's man and her sister saw it. They didn't speak for almost a year after that and that was plenty of time for the enemy to talk Sidney out of the gift of salvation she had received. The thief cometh not but to steal, kill and destroy and he had just about convinced Sidney that her life was not worth living. With no where else to turn she had gone to several doctors and the best they could do was prescribe a bottle of pills with unlimited refills... but God is faithful and now every morning when Sidney woke up she got down on her knees and praised God for His mercy. God saved her life and touched her sister's heart all in the same day. They were able to form an even stronger bond than the one they had previously shared.

Sidney's eyes glistened when she thought about her newly found family. While she was in recovery, the father she had only known for a few months came to visit her in the hospital and surprised her with papers announcing his intention to adopt her. She cried all day long. When they finalized the adoption she changed her last name from Riley, her mother's maiden name to Lyons. The court documents confirmed what she already knew in her heart and what her family had been saying since she joined them. She was a part of them.

After seeing two rock-solid Christian counselors for several months, they suggested she get a new start to go with her new name. She found this church after looking for seven weeks. The people were friendly and the atmosphere felt right so she decided to join the church and settle in. She had been doing well too. At first, some of the members recognized her from the news stories about her defense trial with the rock star but they didn't bother her about it. In fact some even told her that they had been praying for her. She felt like God had blessed her to find this very special church and after everything she had been through, she just wanted to rest.

There's no rest for the weary though. *Not today anyway* she thought as she stretched and yawned and headed for the bathroom.

***

Sidney cradled the phone between her cheek and her shoulder hoping it wouldn't fall into the stew she had just finished. "So what's for dinner?"

Her sister Sidra laughed on the other end. "Well the twins are having cheerios and whatever they'll eat off our plates. The rest of us are having steak with rice and peas."

Sidney smiled knowing that at least one person in the house would not be pleased with the dinner menu. "And what is Miss Kyra going to do with the peas?"

Sidra laughed again. "I don't know. She tried slipping them to her hamster last time but we're on to her now. Leo may actually eat them because he seems to be less discerning than his sisters when it comes to his diet. That boy will shove anything in his mouth given the chance."

"And how is my sweet Jenna doing? I miss her."

Sidra grunted happily. "You just saw her and she's fine, in here following Kyra around the house since she's been home from Sunday school. I'm hoping she'll tire herself out by bedtime."

"Kyra must be a real God-send right now. I know she was when I had them yesterday. I don't think I would have made it through the day without her."

"You know I wasn't sure what to expect when Leslie said she wanted Kyra to move in here full time but all of the kids have adjusted really well."

Sidney put the lid back on her pot of stew and settled into a kitchen chair. "And what about the parents?"

"Oh, we love it. Jensen walks around with a big silly grin saying he's glad to see his 'clan' all together. And I've always looked at her like she was my own daughter. Besides that, you're right; she's been a huge help with the twins. I'm really wishing for a permanent arrangement but I don't want to get my hopes up. I'm not sure what's going on with Leslie right now but I'm going to enjoy this time with the whole family together while we have it. I am a little worried about how this is affecting Ky though. She hasn't said anything but having your mother ship you away to a different household has got to affect you in some way, even if it's your dad's house and you receive love when you get there."

Sidney had wondered the same thing and wandered into her living room while Sidra was speaking. She reached for the remote control and started flipping through channels. "What do you mean you don't know what's going on with Leslie. I thought you all had worked out some type of arrangement for Ky to stay there."

Sidra strapped both babies into their high chairs before reaching for the cereal box and continuing. "Nope, she just called Jensen up at the end of the summer and said she wanted Kyra to move in with us for a while. Of course he jumped at the chance but she didn't offer an explanation then or since then."

"Wow, that seems pretty strange huh?"

"Yeah, and she's still not talking. We're just praying for her since we don't know what else to do."

"Yeah I guess that's best. Have you tried asking Ky about any of it?"

"No, I was trying to give her some space and let her open up on her own."

"I can see that, but maybe she's too scared to talk about it. You might need to help her out."

"You're probably right. Listen, Let me get off this phone and get dinner served. I'll talk to you later and we'll see you next week right?"

Sidney smiled. "I wouldn't miss it for the world, although, I do need to go shopping for a present."

"That's makes two of us."

"What size is little Mike wearing these days anyway?"

"I don't know." Sidra laughed lightly. "Amanda said he's already outgrown all of the 4T clothes he has in his closet."

Sidney smiled. "Do they make husky sizes for soon to be five-year-olds?"

Sidra laughed just thinking about her nephew. He was all cheeks and stomach and couldn't get any cuter if he tried. "I'm not even sure they call it husky anymore. I'm going have to look into that."

"Let me know when you find out." Sidney laughed back. "I was about to order him a size 6."

Sidra shook her head at her sister. "Shopping online again, sis?"

Sidney laughed even harder. "Yes, but I got delivered from the Home Value Channel. Now I only use them online and when I don't have time to shop in the mall, which is most of the time."

"Oh, I bet you're crazy busy. How did the architects in New Orleans like your design?"

"They loved it!" Seeing nothing was on worth watching Sidney turned the T.V. off before heading back to the kitchen. "They're talking about setting up a deal where we'll be working together permanently but we can talk about that later. Go feed your family."

"Alright girl, love you."

"Love you too."

***

Next weekend the whole family got together and partied like rock stars, clean and sober rock stars to celebrate the 5th birthday of Mike's oldest child. Mikey's chubby face lit up in excitement as he spied all the colorfully wrapped presents waiting just for him. The party theme was pirates and when Sidney walked through the door, little Mike jumped on her followed by six other little pirates. Her brother, big Mike had to pull them off of her. "No attacking guests when they come through the front door" he'd said.

"O.K. Daddy" little Mike replied quickly before turning back to his aunt. "Arrrgh! Ahoy there, Auntie. We're pirates!"

Sidney laughed at the rag-a-muffin troupe. "I see that, and such a fine group of pirates too. I don't think I've seen any scarier pirates on the seven seas."

"Aye! We're taking over this place." He pulled a black patch over his left eye, lifted his little plastic sword and let out a menacing yell before he and the other boys took off.

Mike swallowed her up in a hug. "Sorry about that sis. He's been hyper-active ever since we told him he could have this party."

Sidney smiled at her brother. "I would have been concerned if he didn't act like that. It's not everyday a boy turns the big 5."

Mike laughed, "Yeah, I guess you're right. Come on in. Let me take your coat. Everyone is in the kitchen. Sid and her crew arrived a couple of minutes ago."

She found Amanda, Mike's wife, who had announced several weeks earlier that she was expecting again so her little bump was just starting to show. Next she went and spoke to Liz, Sidra's best friend and saw that her son Jaden was growing like a weed. Not as tall as Kyra but still getting big.

Sidney looked around in envy at her siblings as they tied shoelaces and fixed hotdogs and fussed over their families. Even with all the chaos going on around them she could tell they were happy. She couldn't wait for the day when she would be able to bring her own kids to family gatherings.

When all the kids were sent outside to play, Sidra and Sidney joined Amanda at the kitchen table. Amanda reached to give Sidney's hand a quick squeeze. "How's it going sis? I feel like I haven't seen you in forever."

"Everything is good. I've just been a little busy with work."

Amanda slumped down in her chair and yawned. "I guess so with all that traveling but at least you get to come home and rest without anyone bothering you every five minutes. I kind of miss those days, when I could come home and worry about just me."

Sidra joined in with a resounding "Amen!" before the married women shared a high-five.

Sidney was shocked. "Are you two kidding me? I would love to have your lives right now. I would trade my company for a husband and kids any day."

Sidra looked at her sister. "Now that I have them, I wouldn't trade them for anything but let's be clear, this marriage and family business is hard work. I was ready to throw your brother-in-law out the house last week."

Amanda nodded. "Mmhmm, and I almost gave your nephew away the week before that."

Sidney's eyebrows shot up at their honesty. As if on cue, they all started laughing and couldn't stop. They giggled themselves into a fit of near hysteria. Sidney who had been laughing so hard she started crying, wiped the tears out of her eyes before she spoke again. "I know it's hard but I really want a family."

Sidra smiled at her younger sister. "Then I think you should pray and ask God for one. Just don't be surprised if doesn't come the way you're expecting."

A child's howl of pain abruptly ended the conversation and brought all three women to their feet and running into the living room. After the crying child was soothed and the mess that caused the pain was cleaned up, they joined everyone outside and sung happy birthday to the little pirate of the family.

The next week, things were back to normal. All the family birthdays had passed and Sidney was settling back into her normal routine. It was Sunday evening and she was just finishing up a conversation with Kyra and then Sidra. She gurgled to the twins in baby talk before she hung up the phone and fixed herself dinner. As she sat down, she pondered the events of the day. As always, a guest minister had come because it was the last Sunday of the month. This particular preacher was young but he'd been well known in church circles for several years. Things started out like they usually did every Sunday. After the choir finished singing the young man took his position in the pulpit. He had just finished reading the bible verses he was to expound on when he stopped mid-sentence. The visiting minister stared at Sidney for only a moment before he actually stopped the service to point her out and pray for her.

He then proceeded to tell her about the future God had planned for her. He also spoke some things about warfare she didn't quite understand but she soaked it all in just the same.

Mostly everyone in the congregation was stunned. That type of thing just didn't happen at Hearts Desire. Not that they were opposed to it, it just wasn't a regular occurrence. The congregation, however, quickly got over their initial shock and joined the young minister in praying for her. After the service was over, Sidney was surrounded. Most of the people wanted to shake her hand or talk to her. Some even wanted to pray for her again. She was so busy with the people around her that she didn't notice the look of jealousy that sprang up on her pastor's face. He surprised even himself with that reaction but he managed to make it to his office before anyone saw it.

Where he normally would have invited the guest minister into his office for refreshments and a long talk at the end of service, he sent the young man home with a small check and a clap on the back. When the man left, Canaan quickly retreated into his study to pray. He didn't notice Vern, the old church custodian sweeping up in the hallway when he shut his office door.

Sidney returned home that afternoon bubbling with quiet excitement. She sat down in the peaceful house and just marveled at the God who would do such a thing. That visiting preacher had articulated everything she had been carrying around in her heart, even the bits and pieces she had been too afraid to verbalize because they sounded too far out of reach. He hit on every single thing God had previously whispered to her, but he made it real by saying them out loud. She knew then that she had God's stamp of approval. To almost anyone else, the dreams she believed were sent from God would sound absolutely crazy but she chose to believe God. She accepted the words spoken by the preacher as true and contemplated what a very bright future must lie ahead of her. *I believe you God.*

The public have an insatiable curiosity to know everything, except what is worth knowing ~ Oscar Wilde

CHAPTER 2

"Now you know I would rather step on my lips than gossip." Edna-Jane, the church secretary dabbed at the corner of her mouth and swallowed before looking up at her pastor. "But rumor has it that she was an adult film star before she dated the rock star."

"Is that right?" Pastor Canaan Styles studied his secretary as he stood by her desk.

"That's what they say."

"Isn't that something" Canaan always found her little 'member updates' amusing but this one intrigued him more than most. He had just come out of his office to pick up the lunch dropped off by one of his assistants when he stopped by to ask her how she was doing. He knew he was going to hear some idle chatter along with her latest health concerns but she was like the *National Intruder,* the information she offered should always be looked upon as suspect but neither could it be completely discounted.

"Mmmhm, but look how God has turned that thing around. Now she's got preachers calling her out and prophesying over her. Blessed be the name of the Lord! And do you know that my prescription prices jumped up again?"

"Oh, now that is a shame." The pastor barely let her finish her statement before he was walking toward his office. If this latest bit of information turned out to be true, he might think about adding a few dollars to her paycheck. Edna knew how things worked around there and she was used to receiving a little bonus every now and then based on good information. He didn't bother buzzing her when he reached his desk but picked up the church directory and phone himself. He waited patiently until the silence on the other end of the line indicated that someone had picked up.

"This is Officer Walker."

"Hi, yes, Brother Walker, this is Pastor Styles. I had a few quick questions for you. Do you have time to talk?"

The younger man stopped what he was doing and turned his full attention to the phone. He had been attending Hearts Desire for several years and had never received a phone call from the pastor. "Yes of course, anything for you, sir."

Canaan was still in awe at the response people gave him because he was a pastor. After his childhood it had taken him quite a while to understand that most people were kind-hearted, or at least tolerant and not malicious like his father. Several decades later he was more than comfortable with the respect and honor his position afforded him. "Good. This won't take much time. There is a young woman at our church, her name is Sidney Lyons do you know her?"

The younger man nodded and smiled. "Oh yes, we worked together serving the homeless a few times. She's a great person."

"Yes...well, she's applied to work with our youth in the Sunday-School and you know we have to do a background check on all persons wishing to serve in that capacity."

"Right, of course."

"Yes and I know she wants to get started right away so if you wouldn't mind taking care of that I would really appreciate it."

"Sure Pastor. No problem at all. I can get the information back to her in..."

"Uhh, no, no. You can just give me the information. I told her that I... I mean the church would take care of the fee. You just give me the information and I'll let her know when the results come in."

"Will do, Pastor Styles. I'll hand deliver the results to you in a couple of weeks."

"Excellent! Brother Walker, I sure do appreciate you taking the time to do this."

"Like I said, anything for you Pastor."

Canaan hung up the phone and immediately asked God to forgive him for the little white lie he just told. He felt the peace of God but his mother's voice had taken up residence in his head and would not be pushed aside. *If you lie, you'll steal and if you'll steal, you'll kill.* He prayed once more then turned toward the hutch behind him to reach for his pen and paper. He needed to write out the message for Sunday morning and he was already behind schedule. An hour later he finished what he thought was his finest piece of work yet. It was almost as if he had some unseen help working with him to write the message to his people. *Thank you God.*

Canaan reviewed the notes for Sunday's sermon for several more minutes before he locked up his office to head home. He heard the vacuum come to life with a roar just as the lock on his office door set. He dreaded turning around because he knew who would be attached to the handle of that vacuum cleaner but it was time to go home and he didn't want to prolong his time there any longer. *He needs the love of Jesus too, I suppose.*

"Well, hello there Pastor Styles!"

"Well hello yourself Vernon, how are you doing?"

The old man ran his tongue around the inside of his cheek as if he needed to think about the answer. Canaan wondered why it took him so long when he gave the same response every time, "Fair to middling I suppose but I won't complain. Nope, no since in complaining."

Canaan kept walking in hopes of avoiding a longer conversation but it wasn't to be. The older man caught him as he paused to put his coat on. "And how are those two sons of yours, Hophni and Phineas?"

"Those aren't their names and you know it", the pastor seethed.

"Hee Hee, I knows it, just like messin' with you."

"Well I don't find it very amusing brother."

"I'm sorry, Pastor. I just figured I'd make a little joke, helps the time go faster."

"Yes, well speaking of time, mine is getting away and I need to get home. Have a good night Brother Murphy."

"Alright then, goodnight."

Canaan didn't bother to respond. He knew the reference to the seedy biblical characters was meant as an attack against his own children. How dare he talk about his sons like that. Yes, they had a few issues but whose children didn't. Canaan rushed to his sensible car in it's reserved spot. Once in the car he started the motor running then let his mind wander back a decade to when his sons were just boys of nine and ten. His family had accompanied him to a church he had been invited to minister in. His wife had dutifully gone to sit in the front pew to wait for the service to start just as a visiting church's first lady should. She had assumed the boys, Logan and Conner, had taken their seats behind her after a visit to the lavatory.

The boys had actually disappeared down a small, dark corridor in the little church. They found themselves outside the dressing room of the choir where someone had left a tiny crack in the door. They peeked through to see half-dressed women changing into their robes for the performance later that night. So engrossed were the boys in the women's under garments that they did not hear the pastor of the small church walk up behind them. He grabbed them both by the collar and dragged them to the office where their father was waiting.

Once the other man had explained what happened, Canaan was embarrassed to say the least but that pastor's final words stuck with him to this day. "Canaan, I know boys will be boys but you better get ahead of this thing and ahead of them before something potentially harmful happens." *I would have, if I had the time... but I had my church to build* he thought. Besides, he hadn't heard much from that pastor over the years. Shaking his head, Canaan thought back on how everyone had pegged him to be the next up and coming hotshot, the one to watch, but it goes to prove that sometimes people are just wrong.

Young pastor Garvin Temple didn't know it but he had stirred up the wrath of the pre-pubescent Styles boys that day. They held that grudge captive for years with no hope of letting it go. Five years later when the opportunity presented itself, the boys all but murdered the man with their words when someone asked their opinion of him. Like their father, they soon realized that their last name carried a certain amount of weight and they were indiscriminate with the use of it.

They told everyone who asked and some who didn't that Pastor Temple was a closet homosexual and went so far as to imply that he had touched one of them inappropriately when they were small boys visiting the church with their father. The lie changed with the telling and re-telling of the story but they got their point across. Garvin Temple was effectively black balled in the space of a few months. Nothing could have been further from the truth but as Conner told Logan 'gossip and eating are the only things church people are allowed to do.' That was the boys' first taste of power and ever since that day there was nothing they sought after, hungered for and craved quite like they did power. With each lie or manipulation their desire grew stronger until it was only matched by their libidos.

***

Officer Ephraim Walker stopped by the desk of the young rookie who had been assigned to complete the numerous requests for background checks coming into the precinct. He was a little too eager to please and slightly annoying but Walker had made it a point to take the younger man under his wing and mentor him when and where he could. He was even planning on inviting him to church soon because something about the young man's demeanor was crying out for help. Walker had been on the force for ten years by that point and liked to help the rookies out when he could.

"Winston, you got that background check I requested earlier ready for me?"

"Yes sir! I even threw in a little something extra for you." The sly smile Winston gave after the statement told Lt. Walker he should check the file before handing it over to his pastor and he meant to but time got away from him. The file was all but forgotten until it was time to head to prayer meeting. He grabbed the folder off his back seat and stuck it in his bible to stay until he handed it over to Pastor Styles after the service.

"Sir, the results of the background check for Sidney are in here. I haven't had a chance to look at them but everything should be in order. If not, just let me know."

Canaan smiled at his new friend. "I'm sure everything is fine. Thank you brother Walker. I really appreciate this."

The smile Ephraim gave was sincere. "Anything I can do to help, sir."

He happened to walk by Sidney on his way out and stopped to giver her a hug. "You've got great things ahead of you."

Assuming he was talking about the prophecy given a few weeks earlier she smiled back at him and offered her thanks. She had no idea about the background check for the fake position working with the children's ministry...and he had no idea what was in the envelope he had just handed over to Pastor Styles. At that moment, only one person knew and he was busy enjoying the fruits of his own labor.

Winston settled himself on top of his bed and stared at the large glossy black and white photo in front of him. Working on background checks all week was nonsense. He wanted to be out in the field with the rest of the new recruits but he was stuck behind a desk unable to see any of the action. That was, until he pulled the file for Sidney Lyons. He barely glanced at the bulky written file and instead went straight to the large photographs in the back of the file. The naked young woman in the provocative poses grabbed his attention immediately. *This is better than any magazine.* He grabbed two of the photos and slid them into his top desk drawer before he returned the file. He didn't bother to read that the photos weren't real but digitally manipulated by the woman's stalker, or that the man would likely be in a mental institution for the rest of his life. He just grabbed the photos and put them away for safekeeping. *Officer Walker must have been looking out for me.* He stared at the image until he fell asleep determined that he would find Sidney Lyons sometime soon.

Across town, Pastor Canaan Styles was falling head first into the same trap. After he finished up praying for the remaining few who stayed after the church service he made sure the sanctuary was in order before retiring to his office. Forty-five minutes after opening the envelope, he was in the same spot. At his desk, he stared at the picture of what he thought was Sidney recently posing nude for the camera. The picture was proof that Edna-Jean was right. She had been an adult film star. He would have stayed longer had it not been for the ringing phone. "Yes, dear, I'm on my way home soon."

Before he left though, he made a note to include a bonus in Edna's payroll check. He looked at the picture once more before gathering his belongings and heading for home. How could he have known that only a few miles away, the man who had created the bawdy image sat rocking back and forth in a small cell with his arms immobile. Adam didn't mind the straightjacket though. It was the voices that never stopped talking that were making him weary. He continued to converse with them though because he knew what would happen if he stopped.

On Friday Edna opened her check and saw the amount had been bumped up significantly, even far above a normal 'bonus'. She understood what that meant. She picked up the phone right away to get her committee together for an emergency prayer service that night. She had no idea of what actually went on but she knew enough to know that if the pastor rewarded the information she had given him about Sister Lyons, it had to be true. When the ladies met that evening, they discussed the state of affairs over fried chicken and peach cobbler. They must have analyzed the situation every which way before all the women departed for home five hours later.

Edna was conscious to make sure they prayed for the poor lost soul of Sidney Lyons before at least half of the committee members left for the evening. That almost five minutes of prayer was one of the longer ones they had ever done but Edna felt justified that the time-consuming prayer was worth it, given the subject matter.

The next Sunday, Sidney wondered at the looks she was receiving from some of the older women in the congregation but didn't pay it much mind. She had seen first hand at a ministry meeting several months ago how the elderly group of "holy women" could turn into a gaggle of cackling hens in an instant and tried to steer clear of them when she could. Of course her pleasant greeting and quick escape were noted by the group as confirmation of Sister Edna-Jean's careful research, which in turn called for another meeting. The next week Edna made sure everyone else in the office was out of earshot when she picked up the phone. Once the call connected, the telling began.

"Sister, we need to pray, again!"

The doors we open and close each day decide the lives we live ~ Flora Whitemore

CHAPTER 3

Sidney looked at her cousins with her mouth wide open for several seconds.

"You can't be serious?"

Anita and Alisa nodded at her in unison but Alisa spoke up first.

"You know we wouldn't ask you if there was any other way but we have exhausted every possibility."

Sidney stood up and tried to keep her voice calm. "Of course you have. Your mother has issues and no one in their right mind is going to take her in."

Her cousin Alisa looked bewildered. "She's not that bad."

Sidney's eyes grew in circumference with each second that passed. "We're talking about Meena Campbell right? The one who cursed out the entire senior class of a local high school because they came to clean up her yard?"

Anita reached for her cousin's hand. "Sid, please! Aunt Alex said she would take the kids but she didn't have enough room for mama too. You are our last hope. We're both being deployed to Afghanistan in two weeks and she has no where else to go."

Sidney sat back down. "No, it's not going to work. I'll find a senior home or respite care for her."

Alisa's eyes pleaded. "Sidney, please. We can't afford that. We both have to send Auntie Alex money for our kids, not to mention our mortgage payments and paying tuition at their private school. We will have just enough left to send you something for mama but we can't afford another expensive bill like a senior home would charge."

Sidney deflated into the sofa cushion. "Why are they sending siblings into a warzone together anyway? I thought there was a rule against that."

Anita smiled. "There used to be one but now that we're in a war and we don't have as many soldiers as we need, that rule has gotten pushed to the side. Sidney please, they're telling us that it will only be for six months."

"But there's a possibility that you both will be sent back over there after that six months is up isn't there?"

Anita inhaled deeply not wanting to think about that. "It's possible."

"And she can't stay by herself in one of your houses while you're gone."

Alisa reached for her cousin's hand once again. "I'm afraid her failing memory makes that impossible. We're not sure if it's old age or if Alzheimer's is setting in but we can't trust her alone for days at a time. Sidney, I know we're asking a lot of you but you'd really be doing us a great favor."

Sidney sighed one final time. "Fine, I'll do it. I'll set up the guest room down stairs here." Her cousins were so grateful. They thanked her for lifting that burden off of them and hugged her for a long time before they left.

The guest room was spotless and fresh linens were piled high in the closet before Sidney decided to go for a drive. She needed to clear her head and soon after she pulled out of her driveway, her car was headed in a familiar direction. She pulled up in front of her aunt's house and just waited. She was hoping for a sign, some indication that God wouldn't make her go through the valley of the shadow of Meena. She delayed for several minutes but God didn't speak and no storm came to blow her away so she opened her car door and walked up to the porch. Maybe her Aunt Alex could help set her mind at ease. *God knows I'm going to need it with that cantankerous old bitty.*

Aunt Alex was happy to welcome her favorite niece and swung the door wide open. They settled down with some hot tea and pound cake a few moments later.

"Aunt Alex, I don't know if I can do this."

The round graying woman just shook her head from side to side. "Ooohh girl, that's a whole lot of ugly to be puttin' up with … and I'd be wondering the same thing but let me give you a little information that may help you get through it. Your daddy met Meena first, before he met your mama."

Sidney's head almost spun around on her shoulders. "What!"

"Yep, and she was head over heels about that man. They had been seeing each other for about 2 weeks when she brought him home to meet everyone. Oh your daddy was a handsome devil back then but he sure caused some pain in this family. Anyway, she was already making wedding plans by then. 'Course we didn't know he was already married to your sister's mama. Well he walked into the house and took one look at Olivia and decided he wanted her more than Wilameena I guess. He swept Livi off her feet and you were born about a year later."

Sidney's mouth never closed shut after the initial shock wave. "You mean…"

Alexandria nodded. "That's right. Your mama stole Meena's man and she hasn't been the same since. Neither one of them ever came back to themselves after that. Livi was too proud to apologize but I doubt Meena would have accepted it even if she had. Then once we found out that Sidero was married it was too late. Livi was already pregnant with you and Meena never let her live it down. When he disappeared it broke Livi's heart but Meena just grew, well...meaner and she talked about you like a dog when you were born which is why Livi kept you away from most of the family events. We all tried to talk to Meena but she wouldn't hear nothing we had to say."

Sidney who hadn't moved since her aunt started talking took a moment to stretch her neck and lean back slightly. "It all makes since now."

Alex reached for her niece's hand. "Honey, I'm sorry you were born into the circumstances that you were but I'm so glad you're a part of our lives. And it just tickled me to no end when we discovered you had a strong constitution and could put Meena in her place."

Sidney smiled remembering the incident at the family reunion when she was about twelve years of age. Her mom had finally broken down and decided to attend the event after not seeing her family for what seemed like forever. Meena had stared Sidney down with the evil eye all day and had gone out of her way to make Sidney and Olivia feel unwelcomed at the family event, the first one they had shown up to in years. When by the mid-afternoon Sidney couldn't take it anymore, she turned to her mean aunt Meena and said "You know you're not scaring anybody right?" Olivia looked pleasantly surprised but it didn't last long because Meena jumped up and started toward

Sidney. Sidney who already had two inches over her mean aunt by then was ready to take on all comers but her mother and aunt Alex both realized that Meena had one hundred pounds and at least that many months of pent up anger she would have gladly taken out on Sidney and anyone else who got in her way. Alex stopped the rampage while Olivia packed up her daughter and headed home. Alex and her children dropped off two plates loaded with food later that evening.

The older woman chuckled as she relived the memory along with Sidney. "And when Lisa and Anita told me what happened at your sister's house with Meena last Christmas, child they had to pick me up of the floor about 3 times. Looks like you and your sister both got a healthy dose of gumption."

Sidney thought about Sidra and grinned. "That we did. Sidra says we have our grandmother to thank for it."

Alex reached for another mouthful of pound cake before laughing loudly. "Ha! Wish I'd known her. She sounds like a hoot!"

When Sidney spoke to Sidra later that night she heard the microwave buzzer go off just as she finished relaying everything Aunt Alex had told her.

Sidra slammed one warm baby bottle down on the counter before reaching for the other one. "Shut up!"

Sidney was still in shock also. "I know, right? We never stood a chance of being liked by her. Her view of us was tainted from the beginning."

***

Four days later Meena shuffled into the house with the look of disgust she always held when Sidney was around. She looked around the large, nicely decorated townhome wondering how many men Sidney had slept with to afford such a nice place. She couldn't believe the daughter of two such whorish individuals had the capacity to earn anything this nice. The artwork alone probably cost more than what her meager house was worth. But she wouldn't complain, her life had turned out just fine.

After that mess with Sidero she found the most unattractive man she could find and showered him with so much attention, he had no choice but to ask her to marry him. She knew some of her friends talked about her behind her back but at least she could be assured of not having to share him with anyone, especially her wanton sisters. Livi was bad but she knew Alex wasn't any better. No, ever since that incident she knew she only had herself in this world; that is, until ugly Albert came along. *God rest his soul.*

As she walked by the plush furnishings she thought about what type of childhood this girl must have had with only Livi as the sole provider. Albert may have been ugly but he was a hard worker and a good provider. And he was kind. *He doted on his girls like queens.* They weren't as pretty as Sidero's bastard children but they were good girls. Thoughts of her late husband and beloved daughters filled her mind as she slowly made her way through the lower level of the beautiful home. *We might not have had nice things but we were well taken care of.* She barely acknowledged Sidney as they reached the room that would become her temporary home.

She knew the girl didn't want her there anymore than she wanted to be there. *Well*, she thought, *we have that in common.* She tried to remember if she had taken her medicine while she unpacked her bags. Her failing memory was the only reason she was in this mess to begin with. Older people were known for forgetting things so why was she being punished? So she forgot to turn the stove off a couple of times. It's not like she burned the house down, not all of it anyway. She knew her girls were worried about her. That was the only reason she was here. They told her not to worry about the kitchen renovation because they would take care of it as soon as they returned from their assignment with the army.

She filled the last drawer of the marble topped dresser then slammed it shut. She would not stay in the house of *that* man's daughter for one minute longer than she had to.

***

Canaan shoved the lewd picture into his desk drawer just as his youngest son walked into his home office.

"Conner, how many times do I have to tell you to make sure you knock before you come in here? I could have been on the phone in a sensitive counseling session. "

"Oh sorry Dad, I forgot."

Canaan sighed out of frustration. "Did you want something?"

"Umm, just wanted to let you know that Mom said it's time for dinner."

"Oh, well tell your mother I'm very busy. Tell her to just leave a plate in the oven and I'll eat when I can."

"O.K. hey Dad, there's a car show going on downtown next week. Do you want to go?"

"Uh, no son, I'm too busy for that, but you all have fun."

The young man didn't blink. His father was always too busy with something or other to be bothered with his real family. His church family was another matter. They got all his time, free or otherwise. Conner turned around and moved out of the small office closing the door behind him. He never really considered their family a functional one. *You would actually have to like each other and spend time with one another to be considered functional* he thought. At least they looked good together, especially on Sunday mornings.

Canaan waited until he heard his son going down the stairs before he pulled out the picture again. He had stared at it so long he was beginning to feel as if he knew her. Everything in the photo beckoned to him... He even felt himself trying to resist but it was hard. The pastor knew if he didn't do something other men of God would be sucked in by her charms. They wouldn't be able to resist the trap. They may see something about her that God has shown them but they needed to know she wasn't ready, not with her lifestyle the way it was. It would be hard to convince them without proof though. That was all he needed. He needed to get close to her so he could expose what type of person she really was.

The best way to do that eluded him. If he tried to expose her outright, some of the church members may take his approach the wrong way. He would need to gather others to help him. They would have to be trustworthy and dependable. People who wouldn't ask too many questions would work best in this situation. That meant Sister Edna-Jean was out of the running. He thought long and hard. He had developed a good rapport with those in leadership at the church but he would still need to play this one close to his chest. He would only be able to tell one or two people at the most. He just wasn't settled on whom to tell. He sighed again. This would not be an easy task. He would have to take his time and pray about it. The mission he was now undertaking was surely sent by God. There was no doubt in his mind about that. Trusting the Lord to lead him to the right people at the right time was the least he could do.

He went downstairs to eat his dinner, finding comfort in the fact that this was not his battle. This was the Lord's battle and the Lord would take care of it. God wanted this Jezebel exposed as much as he did. He found his wife just finishing her dinner and decided to join her. She smiled at her faithful husband as he sat down.

"Hello darling, I see you finished your work early."

"Not exactly but I thought I would take a break and join you."

"Oh, that was nice of you to think of me and I'm glad you took a break. You work entirely too hard."

"You know how it is when you're building a church dearest, you just have to keep pushing through to the end."

"Yes but even God rested on the seventh day. You need to take time for you. You can only help others when you are at your best."

"That's true dear."

So pleasant was the conversation that Canaan didn't notice the creaky floor board in his office sound an alarm. Conner moved quickly and quietly to his father's desk. There was something about the look on his father's face earlier that he didn't like. He almost looked guilty. Conner thought back over his nineteen years and could honestly say that he had never seen that look on his father's face. It was a look that begged to be investigated further. When he tried the front drawer it opened easily. Everything looked to be in order but seconds of rummaging around closer to the back of the desk yielded the reward he was searching for. He was careful not to disturb anything as he pulled the picture from its' hiding place. He looked at the nude body for a long time before he thought to look at the face attached to it. Something about the woman was familiar but he couldn't put his finger on it for several more moments until...*Sister Lyons?*

Still in shock, he returned the photo to its' original position leaving everything as he had found it. He made his way back down the hallway to his own room where he sat down to think things through. Was it possible that his father was having an affair? Conner knew there were some women in the church who would do anything for a man but she didn't seem the type. The way she looked, she could have had any single man in the church that she wanted. Why would she take up with his father? It couldn't be his physique or his looks. His dad was no blue ribbon winner in the area of attraction. He contemplated it a while longer before the answer came to him. She must be attracted to his power. That was the only thing he could think of that made any sense.

He thought about his father at that moment. He couldn't blame the old man for being interested in the younger woman. His mother was a wonderful woman but Sister Lyons was gorgeous. Any man, especially an older man like his dad, would be flattered by such attention. Most men were weak when it came to beautiful women. He could relate because he had often fallen into the same trap himself. His father really couldn't be blamed.

He stretched out on his bed to ease the tension building in his body. The more he thought about it the angrier he became. His father couldn't be blamed but Sidney Lyons sure could. *How dare she creep into our lives to destroy our family!* He wasn't that close to his father but he would protect his mother with everything in him. Right now it appeared his mother needed protecting from Sidney Lyons. Oh, *she's going to pay for her deceitfulness*. Conner would make sure of it.

***

Sidra surveyed the mess that was her living room and groaned. She was never what some would call a neat freak but even she could no longer take the chaos stacking up around her. The babies' toys were strewn from the front door to the kitchen. She had just put them down for the night and knew if she didn't take care of the clutter now she wouldn't get another chance until the end of the week. The house would likely be featured on the T.V. show *Hoarders* by that time so she made her way into the untidy space and began her organizing.

Jensen joined her in the room a few minutes later absent-mindedly picking up a toy here and there. He had an odd look on his face but didn't say anything.

Sidra smiled at her husband. She had seen that look before. "What's wrong? Did Kyra ask another deep philosophical question?"

He shook his head 'no' as he sat down. When he didn't return her laughter she became worried. He stretched his hand toward her as she moved to stand in front of him. When they were seated side by side he turned to face his lovely wife.

"I'm not sure...I mean I think..." He spent another minute staring at her.

"What? Spit it out already! You're making me nervous."

He took a deep breath and tried again. "I think I heard God speak to me."

Based on his posture and his facial expressions during the last few minutes, Sidra wasn't sure what to expect, but it certainly wasn't this. She took a moment to get herself together before she spoke. "When?"

"Just a few minutes ago when I was in the bathroom." He didn't say anything else, simply sat there looking dazed.

After numerous ticks on the clock passed by she realized she would have to encourage him to continue. "What did He say?"

"That's what I'm not sure about."

"You're not sure you heard correctly? Or is it that you don't really want to deal with what you heard?"

"If I heard correctly, it affects you too."

If she thought the mess in the living room was bothering her, the five-minute pauses between sentences was going to push her over the edge. "Alright, out with it! All cards on the table, right now. Let's go!"

He grinned at her. "I love that about you."

She grinned back. "That's sweet, but you still haven't said anything."

They both laughed and when the laugher subsided he grabbed her hand. "I think I just got called into the ministry."

"Wow" is all she said. Nothing else came to mind.

Nearly all men can stand adversity, but if you want to test a man's character, give him power ~ Abe Lincoln

CHAPTER 4

Sidney finished packing the last box of food for the homeless shelter and turned to gather with her fellow volunteers for the morning. After informing the group that someone would be by to pick up the boxes that afternoon, their leader invited them to join him in prayer for the shelter's residents. They disbanded shortly afterward but one of the girls caught up with Sidney as she was leaving the church.

"Hey Sid, wait up!"

Sidney turned to see a familiar face rushing toward her. She recognized the girl who was a few years younger than her from a couple of the ministry meetings at church. They had hung out together at a few church functions but she didn't know her well, then or now. "Hey Damaris, how are you?"

"I'm good. I just hadn't been able to catch you since the preacher prayed for you but wanted to let you know I've been praying for you since then and I'll keep praying that you accomplish what God wants you to."

Sidney had received several messages like that from church members over the last few weeks so she wasn't surprised. "Thanks. I really appreciate that."

Damaris gave a sincere nod of the head before she continued. "I don't mean to come across the wrong way or anything but something like that would have freaked me out. How are you so calm about it?"

Sidney shrugged "I don't know. It didn't scare me because I already knew what he was talking about. He just spoke everything I had been feeling out loud so I guess God kind of prepared me for it."

The girl nodded as she walked along. "I guess but some of the things he said about where you're going...it's pretty big."

Sidney gave a small smile. "It's impossibly huge but I figure if God wants it done, he'll find a way to get me through it and I may look calm on the outside but I am a little nervous on the inside. Mostly excited but still a little nervous."

"Yeah, I can see how you would be and you're right God will take care of everything. I've got to go but pray for me if you think about it. Take care of yourself."

"I will and you take care too."

Pastor Styles watched the nervous young woman walk into his office slowly. He stood and walked around his desk to pull out a chair for her as she drew closer. "Sister Damaris, please have a seat."

"Thank you Pastor."

"You're welcome, dear. Can I get you something to drink?"

She patted her hair uneasily giving her hands something to do while she tried to stop her mind from racing. "No thank you, Sir."

"So how are you doing?"

"Just fine Sir."

His eyes seemed to bore into her very soul. "Are you sure? Because I hear that you're having some financial difficulty. You've come to our community aid office three times in the last two months to get help paying your bills."

He was so thankful last week for the moment of inspiration that struck him in the wee hours of the morning. It was genius really. The only person who could help him get what he wanted was a person who needed something from him. He checked the church's charity records diligently until he found someone who would fit into his plan. This young woman was desperately in need of financial assistance. She was the right age and the right sex. No one would question a budding friendship between Sister Lyons and this young woman. She was the missing piece of his puzzle. From the looks of things she was primed and ready to go. All he had to do now was secure the deal.

The tears started flowing down her cheeks freely as he knew they would. He pushed the square box of tissue toward his visitor and waited for her to dry the salty tracks on her face.

"It's just that it's been so hard in this economy. I've had to get rid of mostly everything I own to stay afloat and it's still not enough. I've been looking for work but I can't seem to find anything. Either I'm too qualified or I apply too late. Pastor I don't know what to do."

He regarded her for a long moment before speaking. "What if I told you there was a way to earn a nice salary and help me in the process."

Her tears stopped immediately. "I would be so grateful and I would do anything to help you."

That's what I wanted to hear. "Good, very good. You know Sister Sidney Lyons don't you?"

"Oh, yes sir! I just saw her. She's terrific, always very helpful."

"Yes, well, she's being considered for a position here on staff and I need to make sure she's worthy. You understand?"

"I...think so?"

Canaan tried to keep his aggravation in check. "I just need you to keep tabs on her, where she goes, who she hangs out with, that type of thing. But it is extremely important that you don't tell her what you are doing or why. Do you understand?"

Her brown eyes grew as big as saucers. "You want me to spy on her?"

Canaan reached across the large wooden desk to take hold of his guest's frail hand. "My dear little lamb, what I want is to make sure I'm hiring the right person for my staff. You understand that I just can't hire anyone to work at this church. This ministry is very important."

"No, I get that."

"Good, because I also want you to be able to pay your bills on time and to stay in your house and have food to eat and keep your credit score healthy. It is slipping below 600 as we speak. What do you want?"

She looked into unwavering eyes. "I want that too, Pastor."

The toothy smile slowly resurfaced on his face. "Good. I thought so. I just wanted to be sure I could count on you. I'll be in touch with you in the next week or two. "

After she left, Canaan paced back and forth in his office. Last week was the third time a friend and man of God had said something about Sister Lyons. *At least he had enough sense not to say it out loud.* Canaan was still of the mindset that she was nothing more than a pretty face but if God truly wanted to use her, he wanted to know about it. He might even be able to use it to his advantage. He would have even reached out to her if she hadn't been walking around so puffed up about hearing her name blasted across the church a few weeks ago. No, if something was going on with her, he would take his time and find out exactly what it was. He sat down and reviewed his plan regarding her over and over again. He did everything but pray.

***

Officer Walker saw Winston sitting at his desk when he walked by at lunchtime.

"Hey Officer Walker, how's it going?"

"Hey rookie, I can't complain. What have you been up to?"

"Not a lot really. Did you ever look over that information in the background check I gave you a couple of weeks ago?"

"I didn't get the chance but it was for a church thing. I handed it over to my pastor the same day. I'm sure everything was fine. He would have said something if it wasn't." If the younger man's complexion had been light enough, officer Walker would have seen the color rush to his face but his dark brown skin hid it well. "Speaking of which, we have a service every Wednesday and I'm going tonight. I can meet you there if you'd like to check out the church."

Winston thought it over and agreed. If the background check was for a 'church thing' that meant the subject of the background check attended that church. He really wasn't into the church thing but he was eager to meet the woman who had consumed most of his waking thoughts and invaded his dreams every night for the last two weeks. He momentarily forgot about his earlier embarrassment as he pictured her in his mind. With just her picture and the computer on in a dark bedroom, it was easy to let his imagination run wild. He felt a real connection with her and knew that she would feel it too, if they met in person. He agreed to meet the older officer in the lobby of the church thirty minutes before the service started. He was hoping to sit with Sidney tonight.

That evening Sidney was inexplicably irate. It was Wednesday. She normally loved Wednesdays because she always looked forward to praising God and praying with her fellow saints. Today though, she was not looking forward to anything but she went to church in spite of her foul mood, hoping that her outlook would be better by the time she left. As she walked up to the building, she noticed a young man staring at her. He moved toward her quickly and intercepted her path. He was relieved to see she looked just like her photo. *She's hot.*

He stepped between her and the door, put his hands in his pockets and waited for her to say something. When she didn't, he did. "I'm Dirk Winston."

Sidney looked the young man up and down. "That's nice."

He thought he would impress her immediately, just by showing up. After a long awkward silence it was obvious that wasn't going to happen and he wasn't sure how to handle the situation. He hadn't prepared for plan B but knew he had to say something. "I thought maybe we could get together and you know... get to know each other better."

Sidney's right eyebrow perked up. "Better? We don't know each other at all. And I'm sorry but today is not a good day. You'll have to excuse me." She stepped around him and walked into the church without so much as a look back.

She didn't see him struggle to pick up what remained of his dignity...or the anger that overtook him as he walked into the building.

Once inside the church, the songs and prayer soothed her soul but only slightly. She felt a general feeling of heaviness in the atmosphere that was not usually present. She looked around the large room but while some people seemed more distracted than normal, no one else seemed to notice. She settled into her seat and did her best to focus on the ministers in the pulpit, but with each passing minute it became increasingly difficult. She rose with relief when the benediction was pronounced and raced for home.

She rushed right past Officer Walker as he was escorting Officer Winston to the front of the church to meet the pastor. They stood in line for only a couple of minutes, waiting their turn before they were able to speak with him.

Officer Walker stepped forward with a big smile. "Pastor Styles, I'd like you to meet Officer Dirk Winston. He's the young man that handled the background check you requested a couple of weeks ago." Canaan's eyes settled on the younger man's face and noticed the trace of embarrassment that lined his features. He grasped the young officer's hand in a firm and vigorous shake.

Winston began to stammer out an explanation. "Hello sir, I hope...I mean..."

Walker chuckled and gave the young man a heavy-handed pat on the back. "He was asking earlier if everything was alright with the information he'd found. I told him it went straight to you but that you hadn't mentioned that anything was wrong."

Canaan smiled at the young man like he was a long lost friend. In all actuality he was. The pastor sent up a silent thank you when he realized that Dirk Winston was the missing piece to his puzzle. The Lord had provided someone else who could get information on Sidney Lyons without drawing suspicion. "Oh everything was wonderful son, just great. It was just what I needed." Dirk locked eyes with the pastor and some unspoken knowledge passed between them. Dirk felt at home suddenly and gave second thoughts to joining the church. Canaan continued, "How long have you been coming here son?"

Officer Walker smiled broadly. "This is his first night, I invited him at the station."

Canaan reached for the young man's hand. "Well now, we can't let this be the last time. We have need of some strong strapping young men around here. Come on by my office some time this week if you get time. I'd like to get to know you better."

***

Something was wrong. She could feel it. Sidney had been on edge all day even after attending church service last night. Her stomach was churning and she knew something wasn't right but she didn't know what. Meena had been her usual ill tempered self the last few days so that wasn't it but she would've have sworn that the atmosphere around her shifted somehow. Some time during the last few days, things in her life had changed. She couldn't see it, she couldn't point to it but she felt it. The air was somehow thicker, could even be described as heavier. If she didn't know any better she would say she was being watched. It almost felt like when she was being stalked a few years back but in a different manner. This felt more intense. It felt personal somehow and much more serious.

When the phone rang a couple of hours later, Sidney honestly couldn't say she was surprised. She had been waiting for a shoe to drop.

"Ms. Lyons? Hi, it's Russell from Art and Stone down here in New Orleans."

"Oh, yes, Hi Russell, how are you?"

"Well, I'm great but I'm afraid I have some bad news for you."

"Really. What's going on?"

"Well we won't be able to enter into that agreement with you after all. Our board of directors pulled the plug on it this afternoon."

"Wow. Well thanks for letting me know and I'm just curious, did they give a reason?"

"Uh, not really. They just didn't think it was something we should get into."

"Alright, well thanks again."

"No problem and good luck with your future endeavors. I'm sure you're going to do big things."

Sidney shook her head, not in disagreement with his last statement but to clear the cobwebs. "Thanks, Goodbye."

She walked into the kitchen and sat down at the small table with her hands under her chin. She wasn't thinking about anything really. Of course she was disappointed that she wouldn't be able to work with Russell and his brother but she had put her future in God's hands several years ago. She wasn't about to jump ship now.

She stood up and pulled a mug out of the cupboard before reaching for the tea bags in the pantry. Meena chose that moment to waddle through the doorway with a scowl on her face. She stopped in the middle of the floor and glared at her niece. Sidney, who was not in the mood to put up with the old lady, stared back for just a split second before ignoring her altogether.

Meena's next words came out in a hoarse screech. "Are you going to make me some?"

Sidney never bothered to look in her aunt's direction when she replied. "If I had heard you ask for some, I would have. Since you didn't ask but decided to come in here yelling at me, no I don't think I will. You can make it yourself. The tea bags are in the pantry behind you."

"I don't want tea! I want coffee!"

Sidney turned around to look at the dismal old woman in front of her. "Then I'm afraid you're out of luck. There is no coffee in the house."

"You did that on purpose."

Dementia or not, she's about to hear the truth. Sidney opened her mouth to let the old woman have it but the chimes of the doorbell stopped her cold. The sound was as welcome as a bucket of cold water but she gratefully acknowledged that it was necessary to retain order and help her regain self-control. Sidney took a deep breath and removed the acrid string of words that had formed in her mind before addressing her aunt. "Would you go see who's at the door please?"

Meena looked for a moment like she was thinking about telling her niece 'no' but after several seconds the bell rang again and she shuffled toward the front of the house. Sidney heard the front door open and then she heard screams that could wake dead souls. The other shoe had dropped.

When she rushed around the corner, she saw that her aunt looked to be doubled over in pain in front of the open door. Just outside the door were two uniformed military officers.

Sidney sank against the wall. "Oh no."

Meena continued hollering at the top her lungs while one of the officers looked at Sidney. "Ma'am, I'm so sorry. May we come in?" She remembered nodding at the man, remembered seeing one of them try to comfort Meena, who would not be soothed and remembered the other man walking over to her as she leaned against the wall. She couldn't remember much after that. Even days later, she racked her brain and couldn't actually remember hearing the words that stopped her heart and brought her aunt's world to an end. She couldn't recall them but she knew they had been said.

"Petty officers Alisa Campbell and Anita Endicott were killed in a road-side bombing two days ago in Afghanistan. They were being transferred to their new posts when enemy fire hit their vehicle. They were traveling together. Everyone in the vehicle was taken. I'm sorry for your loss ma'am."

The men stayed only a few minutes and left soon after their announcement. They had other families to notify they'd said. Sidney remembered watching them stand to leave and seeing her aunt in despair thinking there was no one to help deal with the notice she'd just received abut her cousins, the one that would change her life forever. They left her to manage a shattered family and the aftermath of it. Left her to deal with her screaming aunt who had now fallen out on the floor. Left her to cope with the destruction their words had caused. She couldn't remember the middle of the visit but she remembered the beginning and the end. She needed to see them leave but had to step over her aunt's now limp and whimpering body to get to the window. She wanted to make sure she wasn't dreaming. In her haze, she thought if she saw the men leave that it would help assure her. She saw them but it brought no comfort. As the car pulled away she remembered thinking *they are off to destroy someone else's life.*

Eventually Meena got up off the floor and got herself together long enough to attend the funeral service. Although a tragedy, the service did allow Sidney to see and spend time with her remaining family members. Uncle Ward had flown in from Arizona. She had never met him before that day. Her grandmother's children were broken up into two sets. The first set consisted of the three children produced with her first husband Henry. Ward, Nicholas and Ella were almost teenagers when their father was killed in a horrible accident. Nicholas passed away several years ago and Ella was unable to make it but at least Uncle Ward was present.

There were about twelve years between her aunts Ella and Alex. Alexandra was the first of the second set of children with the second husband Joe. Alex was the oldest but Wilameena and Olivia quickly followed behind. Three girls were born in just four years. Sidney once heard her mother remark that Grandpa Joe wanted a boy but after three girls he didn't want to risk taking a chance.

The funeral and repast were held at Anita and Alisa's home church. The congregation was small but very friendly. It was remarkable that her cousins even went to church. Their mother, Meena carried so much resentfulness in her heart that she hadn't darkened the doorway of a church for almost forty years. Sidney knew the death of her cousins had thrown everyone for a loop, not the least of which was her Aunt Alex who now had to care for three young children.

One of the cousins was recently divorced and the other was never married. Sidney was hoping that the father of the smaller two would do the right thing and take his children. They clung to him during the funeral as if they were afraid to let him out of their sight. He actually sent money and spent time with them when he could. That was a good thing because Aunt Alex was a force of nature but she was getting older in years and didn't need to be stressed with raising three children. The oldest girl Maya was eight years old with a bit of a smart mouth but an absolute sweetheart. Her father barely acknowledged her existence since Alisa brought her home from the hospital. Sidney thought she might even take the girl in if she ever stopped traveling so much.

All things considered, it was a god day. Sidra brought her family to pay their respects and Sidney was happy to see that Kyra and Maya hit it off. Even Aunt Meena seemed to be a little more mellow that day; like she had come to the realization that life was too short to waste on being angry all the time. Sidney was sure that her mean aunt's change in attitude had something to do with the eulogy.

Pastor Garvin Temple preached like they were burying his own family members. Everyone in the room was moved by his words. "Love is the most important thing," he'd said. "We all have several opportunities a day to be offended but if you don't love your way through those opportunities, you will live a very sad and defeated life. Those girls died knowing they were loved, but more importantly, they died knowing how to love."

Sidney could see her aunt was touched by the message. Everyone in the small church was affected, as evidenced by the large number of people surrounding the altar when Pastor Temple extended the invitation to become a Christian. For a moment, Sidney thought Meena might walk down to the front of the church. But she didn't.

Meena kept to herself for the next few days. She did a lot of soul searching during that time. In some ways, she was expecting something like this to happen, expecting God to punish her for the way she had chosen to live. She looked back over her life and knew the words the preacher spoke at the funeral were true. Her daughters had somehow moved past the bitterness she had raised them in, no doubt because of their father and had grown into women that knew how to love.

Meena knew she didn't know how and feared she would never learn. She had treated every one of her family members with apathy and disdain and was now living with a niece whom she was certain would put her out of the house any day now. *Why would she keep me here after the way I treated her?*

Meena thought about her late sister also. She and Olivia had actually been very close before Sidero came into their lives. That is the part that hurt the most she decided. Had she been betrayed by someone she didn't like or even someone she barely tolerated, she could have dealt with that, but her baby sister? The sister she had held in the middle of the night during thunderstorms and fought for and cleaned up after was her betrayer and she didn't know how to move past it. So she stayed there in the hurt and pain and bitterness for almost forty years. *And look what it cost me.*

She didn't even know Livi was sick before she passed away. Of course when she found out, she was too proud to go to the funeral. That's what she told herself, that her pride couldn't stand it but she knew there was some guilt there too. She felt partly responsible for her sister's death because she had heard her nurse friends say that cancer patients who were experiencing personal trauma or even family drama in their lives, didn't seem to recover as well or as often as those who were able to stay joyful during their healing process. Meena knew she was partly to blame for Livi's death and now God was punishing her for what she had done. She couldn't blame Him. *I deserve it* was the last thought that drifted across her mind before she fell asleep that night.

The subsequent days were hard to bear though. For several days she tried to be nicer to Sidney but doubt and fear about her future overtook her and once again she did the only thing she knew how to do. She lashed out at those closest to her.

***

Edna looked the scrawny young policeman up and down. Something about him was not right but she had bigger fish to fry. She buzzed the intercom in the pastor's office to inform him that he had a visitor. "Officer Dirk Winston is here to see you."

Canaan almost jumped straight out of his chair he was so excited. "Oh, yes, please send him in."

Dirk walked in and took a long look around before taking three steps forward and extending his hand. *If preachers are rolling like this, I'm in the wrong business.* "Hi, Pastor Styles."

Canaan grabbed the younger man's hand with great fervor. "Dirk, my boy! Come on in and have a seat."

"I hope you don't mind me coming at this time. It's just that I was on my lunch break."

"Not at all. After two weeks passed, I didn't think you were coming at all."

"Oh, I was just busy."

The pastor smiled. "I see. Well, I'm glad you found the time. That was great work you did on the background check."

The young man cleared his throat in an attempt to push back the tide of embarrassment he felt washing over him. "Oh, thanks. I wouldn't have put that picture in there if I knew you were going to see it."

"Actually, I needed to see that." The good reverend neglected to mention that he'd needed to see it, stare at it, review it and commit it to memory every day since then, also. "You see the reason for the background check was to make sure she was fit to be a part of this ministry."

"Well, uh, judging by that picture, I don't know if ministry is what she is interested in but I guess people can change."

The pastor smiled and nodded. "That's just it. I need to make sure. I need more proof to show exactly what she's into."

The young officer was slowly starting to catch on. "Okay?"

"That's where you come in. I need your help to determine whether she's worthy of being a minister here."

Dirk leaned back in his chair. He hadn't been to church since he was a child, and then only a handful of times but he'd always thought God did the deciding. *Guess things have changed.* "What do you want me to do?"

Canaan reached into his desk drawer and pulled out a notepad. "It's all on here. I just want you to keep tabs on her. Track where she goes and how long she stays, that type of thing. I know this could potentially take up a lot of your time, so I'm willing to pay you. And I just need the information, you won't have to spend any time with her."

Memories of the night he met Sidney came rushing back. "That's good, because she blew me off the last time I saw her."

The older man shook his head. "You see, that's what I'm talking about. Those are the types of things I need to know. If she won't talk to young men at church, who is she talking to?"

Winston shrugged. "She's rude and stuck-up if you ask me but I'll do it."

"Very good. Everything is spelled out on the pad there but feel free to call and let me know if you have any questions later."

"OK, Rev. Nice talking to you."

Both men stood and walked to the door before shaking. "You too son. Take care and I look forward to hearing from you."

"Yes sir."

Canaan knew that almost everything was in place. The missing pieces were coming together nicely. He needed to talk to only one more person and he would soon show them all what Sidney Lyons was really like. She may have fooled everyone else but he was on to her. He walked around his desk and sat down with a thud. Writing sermons used to be the easiest part of pastoring for him. But lately it took everything in him to even feel like writing or reading anything from the bible. It took almost five hours last week and that was unheard of for him. He stretched the length of his body and closed his eyes. He thought about praying but when no words came to mind he simply opened his eyes and decided to write something.

Winston smiled to himself as he settled into his car to drive back to the police station. *So little miss perfect isn't so perfect after all.* He would be happy to bring her down a notch or two. He hated when people thought they were better than everyone else. He laughed to himself. If he'd known the pastor was willing to pay for checking up on her, he would have waited to phone those architects in New Orleans to tell them that she was a recovering addict and he was her parole officer calling to make sure nothing happened 'like the last time she was out of town'.

He'd managed to get a hold of her phone records from a friend who worked for the communications giant that serviced her home and business. She didn't need to go to New Orleans to work with two single men when she could stay home and work. There were plenty of single men in the D.C. Metro area. He knew because he was one of them.

***

Her aunt's apparent epiphany from the funeral was short lived because she was back to her disagreeable self two weeks later, so Sidney watched in awe as Meena rolled around on the floor laughing and playing with her grandchildren. Alex had dropped them off earlier but as was her older aunt's custom when Meena was around, Alex left soon after. The kids screamed and giggled in delight as Meena searched for, ran after then tickled them until they couldn't stand it any longer, falling down on the ground. Sidney sat in a corner, out of sight but quietly observing. "Maybe I should bring the kids to live here, seems like it would make for a happier household," she muttered to herself. She wondered if her aunt would want to continue staying with her at all but hadn't brought the subject up.

She honestly wasn't sure she wanted to deal with Meena for the rest of her life. But Sidney no longer had the luxury of thinking just of herself. Her Aunt Alex had informed her before leaving that morning that Nia and Nico's father Frank would be taking custody of them in the next two weeks. That would have been wonderful news except for the fact that he would be moving two states away for his job. He promised to bring the kids when he could but Sidney knew, a single parent with his schedule would have a hard enough time just getting them clothed, fed and to and from school on time, much less driving six hours to see his dead ex-wife's relatives. Meena would surely miss her two grandkids when they left.

She sighed again. Things were changing swiftly. It almost felt like everything was moving too fast. Sidney would love for her world to stop spinning long enough for her to get off and take a deep breath but she knew there was no such thing. She was going to have to deal with her reality just like everyone else in the world going through hard times.

"Auntie Sidney, come and play!" Maya screamed from the living room.

Sidney peaked around the corner with one eyebrow arched. "Are you sure you want me to come and play?"

"Yes!" Three small voices yelled out in unison.

"OK, but you should know, that if I catch you, I don't stop tickling ever!"

The children answered with more screams and ran for their lives. Sidney was on her way to the living room when the phone rang. Brother Smiley was on the other end. He had been waiting at the church for her to start a meeting with the new recruits for the ministry to the homeless. With everything going on, Sidney had completely forgotten about the meeting she had set up a month ago. She explained her situation; that she was with family and wouldn't be able to get away right now and offered her sincerest apology. Mr. Smiley was very understanding when he hung up.

Pastor Canaan, however, had noticed that she was supposed to be in the building and sauntered over to the room to see what she would be doing. When Brother Smiley announced that he would be conducting the meeting alone, Canaan grew annoyed. He had wanted to see her... or, rather to see what she would be doing. He mentally shook himself. It didn't matter. It was just another check on his list against her. He would show every one who had pointed her out that she was nothing special.

On the way back to his office he wondered what she was doing and decided she was probably out with some man. He had no idea that the object of his derision was at home playing hide-and-seek.

***

Canaan handed the small notepad to Damaris as he walked past her to sit behind his desk. "We don't have a lot of time because I have a counseling session in ten minutes and then a speaking engagement later this evening. Here are a list of her banking, email and social networking accounts along with all of the passwords. I want to know everyone she knows. I want to know everyone she communicates with on a regular basis or otherwise. I want to know where she's getting her money from and what she's spending it on, even the movies she's watching and books she's reading.

I expect a weekly report on my desk by the close of business every Friday.

He spoke hurriedly. "In return you will receive $375.00 every week. That's an extra $1500.00 dollars a month. That should help out with your bills shouldn't it?"

The smile she flashed back was glowing. "Yes, pastor, it definitely will."

"Good, now don't forget. Every Friday."

"No sir, I won't forget."

Damaris almost skipped out of the office. When she closed the door, Canaan just leaned back and sighed. If he thought there was something special about Sidney Lyons, she had proven him wrong a few days ago when she didn't show up for the ministry meeting that she initiated. She was just an ordinary girl who no more had the call of God on her life than the oriole outside his window. How she managed to convince almost everyone else that she was exceptional he didn't know. But he would show them. He would show them all that she was nothing special.

He contacted a deacon who had been with him since the beginning. The man had actually been there when his father had served as pastor and Canaan learned that he was the man to call when you needed anything. He took care of any and everything a pastor may have needed but couldn't or shouldn't get himself. "Whatever you do, keep your hands clean" is what the deacon always told his father and now Canaan. The deacon called in a huge favor to one of the members who was a part of some secret government agency. The brother couldn't even disclose which agency but he had come through with every social networking and bank account registered in Sidney's name along with the passwords. He also provided the contact list on her computer and software to track when she made any changes. Canaan had shared the information with Winston knowing that the young man would keep his confidence.

Canaan smiled at the thought of wiping those so-called prophecies off the lips of those false prophets. He would prove that they were only focused on a pretty face and nice body. He would show them that God wouldn't put those kinds of gifts in a vessel like that. *It wouldn't make any sense to do so.*

On his way out of the office, Edna called out after him. "I've ordered some flowers to send to Ms. Lyons home."

"What?" He stopped on his way out the door. "Why would you do that?"

"Her two cousins were killed in a road-side bombing in Afghanistan a couple of weeks ago."

"Oh." Canaan hurried down the corridor but spoke over his shoulder to his secretary. "Well, don't worry about the delivery. I'll take care of it."

"Edna just stared after the man with her mouth agape. He had never done such a thing before but now he needed to deliver flowers to an ex-porn star personally? Not on her watch. *I see we need to call another prayer meeting.*

...But the hearts of men are easily corrupted ~ J.R. Tolkien

CHAPTER 5

The doorbell had rung twice and the impatient person on the outside was about ready to push it again when Meena ambled over with the help of her cane. She figured it had to be someone for that so-called niece of hers because both her children were with Jesus now and she knew Alex wouldn't bring the grandkids two days in a row for a visit. She knew she was right when she opened the door and saw a man she didn't recognize. "She ain't here. You may as well come back later."

"Mrs. Wilameena Riley? Actually, I came by to see you. It is a pleasure to meet you."

Meena considered the man before her. She was used to making snap decisions and sizing people up in a matter of seconds. After that fiasco in her early twenties, she made a promise to herself that she would never be played for a fool again. She had been studying people and their actions for so long that it became like second nature to her. The ordinary man in front of her was harmless. She would have testified in court about it had someone asked her.

"And you are?"

"Oh, forgive my manners ma'am. My name is Canaan Styles and I'm pastor of the church that your dear niece is a part of." He threw the word "dear" in to feel her out. It seemed that Sidney Lyons was the type of person you either loved or hated. He had gotten some background information on Sidney's aunt from Damaris the night before and found out that she was a pill. Usually, though, blood ran thicker than water so he made sure to test her before proceeding.

"Well, you're one for three. You got the first name right but Riley is my maiden name. I gave that up when I married my dear departed husband Albert, God rest his soul. My name is Wilameena Campbell. And just so you know, that niece of mine is not the dear everyone thinks she is."

Bingo! Canaan rewarded her with his best pastoral smile

"Yes ma'am Mrs. Campbell. I just wanted to drop by and pay my respects. These flowers here are from the church. I understand that both your daughters were taken away in the road-side bombing there in Afghanistan last week."

The far-away look in the woman's eyes threatened to take over and Canaan felt for a moment like she might need real ministry. He fought with himself though because he had a mission to accomplish and he didn't have time to spend with the old woman just yet. He just needed to know if he could count her in the 'for' or 'against' column, then he needed to be on his way. But he knew by the look on her face that he would be there longer than planned...

Thirty minutes later Canaan gathered his coat and stood up. "Don't be too hard on your niece Mrs. Campbell, after all, not all of us have an easy time aspiring to the call of God on our lives."

"Call of God? Humph! That girl ain't a bit more called by God than the man on the moon."

My thoughts exactly. He managed though to at least keep that thought to himself and say the right thing. "Well God is calling all of us to something. You know, I would love to have you visit the church some time in the near future Mrs. Campbell. You don't mind if I call you every now and then just to check on you, do you?"

Canaan buckled his seat belt as he drove away. His plan was coming together nicely, almost too easily. It was as if God wanted this imposter exposed as much as he did. He moved quickly down the road, his car engine racing as fast as his brain. He began mumbling to himself to organize his thoughts. He needed to hurry and get to his office to write out the sermon for this week. It was taking him longer and longer every week to find something to say to address the congregation. It was quickly becoming a chore he could do without. He even considered calling in a guest minister. The problem with that idea was anyone he'd call would be sure to point out Sister Lyons. *Unless you call the Reverend from your seminary,* the thought popped in his head so quickly he knew it must be inspired.

"Of course! Reverend Fitzhugh would be glad to come and minister one of his dry sermons to my church, for the offering he would receive if nothing else." The man was known for his aversion to Spirit-filled assemblies so it was unlikely he would see anything out of the ordinary with Sidney Lyons or anyone else for that matter. Canaan hated to put his congregation through what he knew would be an extremely dry and boring Sunday church service, but it had to be done. He needed to concentrate on other things and right now writing sermons was only puling his focus away from his true mission right now.

By Saturday night everything was in place. Rev. Fitzhugh was scheduled to arrive the next morning with sermon in hand and Canaan had spoken with Mrs. Campbell, Sidney's aunt about coming by the church the next day for a visit. He pulled out the frayed picture hidden in the back of his desk to study it once more. He just couldn't wait to show everyone the truth about her. He knew it wouldn't be long now. With Sister Damaris and Brother Dirk Winston in place, this would be a relatively short operation; he could then get back to tending his church.

Everything went off without a hitch on Sunday. The right reverend Fitzhugh was more impressed with the building than anything else he saw. Canaan did notice a few of his members dozing off during the message but most tried to encourage the older man with nods and shouts of 'amen!' Even Ms. Meena was in the house sitting next to her niece. Meena gave the pastor a nod of acknowledgement after the visiting minister sat down. Canaan looked around and gave God a shout of thanks. All was right with his world again.

After the service was over Canaan invited Rev. Fitzhugh into his office. The old teacher looked around as if he were impressed.

"You know Styles, you've done a major thing here. I have to admit, I didn't expect much from you based on what I saw when you were in seminary."

Canaan offered the man a seat and started toward the wet bar to fix him something to drink. "How's that Professor?"

"Well you know, you were always shouting and carrying on in our chapel services. And you always had your head in the clouds. Too heaven focused to be any earthly good."

"Well, I guess it turned out alright for me."

"I'll say. You did well for yourself."

""Yes sir, I did."

"I see you've even attracted one of those freaks here."

Canaan stopped pouring into the glass he was holding to turn and look at the man. "Excuse me?"

"Oh come on son, don't tell me you don't know about the freaks?"

"Uh, no sir, I'm afraid I don't"

"Well son, who have you been having come preach here, the peanut gallery? Listen, that girl in the gold, she was sitting next to an old woman, I wouldn't mind getting to know, if you catch my drift, anyway, she's one of them. I can spot 'em a mile away."

The curious pastor walked back with a drink in each hand before joining Rev. Fitzhugh. He knew the man was talking about Sidney but honestly thought he hadn't noticed her in the church. The fact that he did notice her was surprising but he apparently knew something else that Canaan needed to know. "I really have no idea what you're talking about."

The old man grunted and mumbled something about giving Canaan too much credit but he wouldn't stop questioning the old professor until he told him everything.

"Well son, it's like this. There are churches all over the country that are putting up with these 'know-it-all members'. Trust me, if she hasn't come to you with a 'word from the Lord', she will. I bet you've already had some visiting preacher point her out already, haven't you?"

Or three, Canaan thought to himself.

"Yeah, judging by your expression I see I have arrived just in time. The bad news is these freaks are everywhere, I mean all over the place."

"Why do you call them freaks?"

"Well son, they're not normal. That's the best way I can say it. They know stuff they shouldn't, like way before it happens or they do things that don't make sense. I've even seen some of them do a freak move and convince the weak minded around them that it was a miracle. Everyone knows miracles only happened in biblical times so God could get through to the people back then. Everyone knows that with the day and age we live in, that we don't need those types of things anymore. It's all of the devil if you ask me. Also, they walk around with their noses up in the air, like they're better than us, every single one of them."

Canaan was transfixed. "And you say this is happening all over?"

"Yes son, I'm afraid so, but there's no need to worry." The man smiled and Canaan grew worried. He looked like something out of a Saturday morning cartoon. "We've developed a system to keep them in check."

"What type of system?"

"Reconnaissance, that's what!" His eyes were wild now and he was practically dancing in his seat.

"Here's what I want you to do. There's a shop downtown near "M" Street, go there tomorrow and purchase a GPS unit, some keystroke software and five or six micro cameras. Find a way into her home, it doesn't matter how but you keep your hands clean. Get one of your more expendable members to do it for you if you have to. Place the GPS tracker under her car, the software on her computer and the camera's in her home and you will know what she's up to at all times. Easy as pie." He smiled, letting Canaan know just how proud he was of himself.

The pastor sat thoughtfully for a few moments until a thought popped in his head. "What if she goes somewhere to get her car checked on, like a service station?"

The man's smile became broader. "That's why you have men in your church to serve you. I'm looking around at what you've built here and I know you didn't get here overnight. You must have some men loyal to you by now don't you? Get them together, only men that you can trust to keep their mouths shut, and deputize them. Give them just enough information to operate but keep them in the dark as much as possible. When she goes to get her car looked at, you call one and tell him to head over there. Tell him to speak to the mechanics first, say something like 'oh you're working on my niece's car, yeah, it's funny my brother still wants to keep track of her at this age' then make sure he speaks to the girl while everyone is watching. It's simple."

When Rev. Fitzhugh left, Canaan wanted to run around the building. God had blessed him with everything he needed to accomplish his goal. The last thing his old professor said as he walked out was a reminder to "keep your hands clean."

***

The black car circled the parking lot until the driver saw what he was looking for. Sidney's car was parked in the back of the lot but there were several cars around her car. He didn't want to take a chance so he waited patiently until one of the cars parked next to hers pulled out. He pulled into the empty space quickly and when he was sure he wouldn't be seen, he got out of the car and placed a small tracking device on the underside of Sidney's car. For some reason the magnet on the device wouldn't catch properly at first so he spent more time than he should have doing adjustments. When an older couple walked by noticed him fiddling around, Officer Dirk Watson just smiled and nodded.

"My wife's car. Thought I saw some oil leaking at the last spot we stopped at."

The lady smiled back. "Oh, that's nice. You don't see a lot of that anymore."

Her husband nodded as they moved on. "Too many selfish people in the world now-a-days."

He had just enough time to make sure the device was secure before he hopped in his car and drove off. He saw Sidney exiting the store as he pulled out of the parking lot.

He dialed his cell phone to call his new pastor. "The equipment is secure and should be live. You can go online and track her in real time now."

When Canaan logged on to the website, it was just as Dirk had said. He saw a little blip representing Sidney's car. He was so happy he had enlisted the services of the young man. Dirk knew the new computer technology so well. Canaan thought he never would have been able to figure out everything so quickly. Dirk, however, was so clever and showed him just what was needed. The equipment was set up in a matter of minutes. Now Canaan could trace her every step. He had access to every bank account and social networking account she owned so he could see exactly what she was up to. It was only a matter of time now before he would expose her for what she really was.

When the next Saturday rolled around, Canaan noticed that Sidney's car was not at her home address. When he pulled up the map, it showed that she had traveled about 35 minutes away to a large shopping mall. He saw the car stop so he figured he had time to accomplish what he needed to while she was shopping or doing whatever it was she was doing. He grabbed his coat and headed out the door.

Three minutes later his youngest son Conner strolled into his father's office and sat down behind his father's desk. When he pulled up the browser history he saw the tracking page. One minute later he had guessed and entered his father's password. Seeing the blip of the tracking device, he guessed correctly that the car belonged to Sidney. He guessed incorrectly, however, that his father was going to meet her at a hotel near where her car was stopped. After digging a little further, Conner found the list of email and social networking accounts associated with Sidney's name, along with their passwords. He copied the lists, the GPS tracking site URL and the nude picture of her and went back to his room. He then set his plan in motion to destroy everything in her life.

***

Sidney looked down at her coat pocket where her vibrating phone was doing a dance. When she pulled it out, she noticed the Facebook notification.

Sidra stopped mid-step to look back at her sister. "Is everything alright?"

Sidney looked up from the handset in her palm. "Yeah, strange though, my pastor's son just friended me on Facebook."

"Oh? Do you know him well?"

"Not at all."

"Hmm, well I guess it couldn't hurt anything. Now come on we've got stores to hit!"

Sidney laughed at her sister. "And they say I'm the bad one."

"Um, usually you are. But I'm on a mission. I've got three kids at home who are determined to outgrow everything I buy them by the end of each month"

"And how is it that you managed to get out of the house without the crew this morning?"

Sidra flashed a wicked smile. "That was the easy part. I just did a little negotiating with my husband but don't worry, he'll get his tonight."

Sidney's face suddenly scrunched up. "TMI, sis."

"Hey you asked." Sidra laughed. "Now come on."

Sidney nodded. "OK, but let's stop by that gourmet shop on the way to the kid's shop. I want to get something for Aunt Meena."

"Really? Wow, I'm proud of you." Sidra was genuinely surprised and gave a sincere smile to her sister.

Sidney grinned back. "You should be, but I think we're both trying a little harder since the funeral. She even went to church with me last Sunday and joined."

"What? Jesus is real!"

"You can say that again. I think she's finally coming around."

***

"Ms. Wilameena, how are you doing?" Canaan beamed down at his newest church member.

Meena stepped aside to let the man in. In all honesty she didn't want any visitors but since he was close to God and she had a lot in her past to make up for, she welcomed him in, hoping her association with him would give her some brownie points with the man upstairs. "Oh, I'm fine Pastor Styles, how are you doing? And I'm afraid you missed her again. She left a little while ago and I'm not sure when she'll be back."

"Oh, that's fine, I actually came by to see you, I wanted to check on you and see how you were doing in your hour of bereavement and I also wanted to talk to you about some things."

"Oh?" Meena looked at the young pastor and wondered what kind of things he could have to talk to her about. "Well come on in, I'll make you some tea."

It was only when the tea set lay nicely on the coffee table and his coat lay neatly on the back of the chair did he begin.

"I'm not sure where to start and I honestly don't know where else to turn. It's about your niece."

The lines above her brow deepened. "What about her?"

"Well, it appears that she may be in some kind of trouble."

Meena paused considering his words. "What type of trouble?"

He kept a straight face when he peered deep into her eyes. "She's being followed by law enforcement."

"What?"

He nodded "Yes" then nodded again. "Yes, I'm afraid it's true." He conveniently left out of the part of story that told how he was the reason she was being followed. "One of my members that work in law enforcement came to me last week with all sorts of accusations about what she may be involved in. He said they were going to bring her in for questioning but I convinced them not to do that. She's already been in trouble once and this wouldn't look good on her record."

"But she was found innocent the first time."

He took her frail hand in his. "Yes but you know how people talk. She'll be much better off if this doesn't go public."

Meena sat quietly with her mind spinning. *I knew she couldn't have gotten this house and all of these nice things legally. No good hussy.*

Canaan sensing that his words had hit their target decided to go in for the kill. "I don't know what she may be involved in but whatever it is, she's in way over her head. Even if she's innocent and just involved with the wrong people, she still has to convince law enforcement of that. It's possible that she could even be looking at jail time for her actions and while I'm hoping that's not the case I thought I would come see you because there may be a way to handle this mess quietly. After all if she's sent away, where does that leave you?"

Meena sat quietly for several moments. Is this what her future had come to? Left with someone she barely knew to care for her in her old age. What was left of her family was taken away from her by a group of terrorists in a country half way around the world. Her sister Olivia was dead but even had she been alive they likely wouldn't be speaking now. She knew she had reeked enough havoc in her sister Alex's life so that she also was no longer welcome there.

She thought about Olivia again. She should have forgiven her younger sister before she died of cancer. Olivia raised this girl all alone and look how she had turned out. Involved in a life of crime all because she didn't have family around her growing up. The girl whom Meena had despised for all of her life now became an object of pity to her. The least she could do was honor her dead sisters memory and try to help this child.

Sidney may not have her mother here but Meena would see to it that she was looked after. She would do what she could for Olivia's sake, at least that's what she told herself. Honor was one part of her motive but fear also played a part in Meena's decision. If the girl were put away she would have nowhere to go. She didn't want to die alone in a nursing home.

"What do I need to do?"

Canaan breathed a sigh of relief when he heard those words. He wasn't completely sure his fabricated story would go over on the older woman but was glad to find out it had worked. "I have a few trust-worthy men that work with me at the church. Let us keep an eye on things. We'll monitor her comings and goings to know for sure whether there is any illegal activity. We can even set it up so that you'll be the first to know what's going with her, that way you can contact us and we can assure the authorities that all is well. You just contact me when anything is out of the ordinary and I or one of my members will try to keep her on the straight and narrow."

Meena listened intently. That didn't seem too bad. If all they needed was access, she could provide that. "All right, how should we handle it?"

He could hardly contain himself. His plan was in motion and he was ecstatic. "I need you to get her out of the house for a while so we can set things up. Call me when you leave and then leave a key to the front door in an easily accessible place. I will take care of the rest."

Sidney arrived home several hours later with a smile on her face. Spending time with her sister always put her in a good mood. She had only been in the house for a few minutes when Meena came in to talk to her.

"We need to go to the store later."

"Sure, no problem. What do you need?"

"I need some coffee. That weak tea you drink is driving me crazy."

Sidney's face beamed as she reached down into one of the shopping bags near her feet. "There's no need to go out Aunt Meena. I picked up some gourmet coffee for you while I was out."

Her aunt was momentarily stunned. "Well...I still need to get some other things."

"Oh, OK. That's no problem. You just let me know when you're ready to go."

"OK, I'll let you know later today."

True to his word, Canaan took care of everything when he received Meena's call. He and Dirk entered Sidney's home with the key she left under the doormat and an hour or so later the house was under surveillance with keystroke software on her computer, tiny pinpoint sized cameras and miniature microphones scattered throughout the house. The software installed on Sidney's computer that would transmit every keystroke directly to Canaan's computer. With the house being monitored and the GPS unit firmly in place, Sidney literally could not make a move without Canaan knowing about it. That was just the way he wanted it.

The next time Sidney left the house, Canaan gave Meena a tutorial on the surveillance system. When he left, Meena felt empowered. She would no longer be subject to Sidney's short or curt answers.

If she wanted to know what the girl was up to, she could just go on the computer and look.

***

Two months later Sidney stomped around the house in frustration. She could be forgetful at times, a lot of people were but she clearly remembered putting the specific piece of jewelry she was searching for in a certain place and it wasn't there now. In fact, several things seemed to be missing over the last few weeks from jewelry to make-up items to toiletries.

In fact, she mused, things in her life hadn't been right for a while. Where she normally would have gotten six or seven calls from potential customers in the last month about her interior-design business, there where none. Her income stream was starting to dwindle and she was feeling the pinch. And then there were those odd moments when her aunt would confront her about things she should not have known like an item she bought or a bill that was due. She noticed the confrontations came right around the time a bank statement or a reminder from customer service arrived in her email inbox. Her password would also stop working intermittently. There were other things too but for now they only added up to one big annoyance. Like right now, not being able to find her bracelet was just another one in a long string of annoyances. She knew Meena was getting older and more forgetful but she had no reason to take her things. *At least she's calmed down some since she started going to church.*

"Aunt Meena, have you seen my gold bracelet, the one with the pearls?"

"No child, I haven't. Did you look in the last place you had it last?"

Sidney was going through the house frantically. Not that the bracelet was of great importance but she knew she had seen it a few days ago in the little silver dish near the back of her dresser. It was almost like the thing had gotten up and walked away on it's own. She knew her Aunt had no use for the bracelet and she couldn't imagine her lying about it but the fact remained that the bracelet was gone.

The next day, Meena was bent over looking under the sofa cushions when Sidney walked into the well-decorated living room. "Aunt Meena did you misplace something?"

Meena looked up and around the room before turning to her niece. "We're missing some forks. You didn't take any out of the house for a church function did you?"

Sidney shook her head. "No. I haven't had a need for them outside of the house."

Meena slowly got down on her hands and knees and looked up and down the length of the sofa. Silverware just doesn't get up and walk out the house by itself. She had taken the dishes out of the dishwasher earlier and noticed that after counting the ones in the drawer and the ones that were just washed, there were only five forks. There was exactly eight of everything else. Eight knives and eight spoons along with the full number of serving utensils filled up the drawer but she couldn't for the life of her think where those three forks could have gotten to. Sidney just shrugged her shoulders. She didn't know where they were either.

Damaris called later that evening. They decided to meet at the movie theatre the next night to hang out. Sidney hung up the phone several minutes later and wondered about her new companion. She had never before felt like she was being interviewed when starting a new friendship. *Oh well, I guess she's just curious.*

All our words are but crumbs that fall down from the feast of the mind ~ Khalil Gibran

CHAPTER 6

Things were perfect in Pastor Styles' world for several months but as is necessary for growth, everything must change. He still hadn't caught Sidney doing anything wrong but he knew she would slip up at some point. He watched her every move while she was in the house and tracked her every move outside the house but there was nothing to show for it. In fact the only vice he could see was she liked to shop but he didn't know a woman who didn't.

Canaan closed his office door and sat down behind his desk. He had just finished reviewing Damaris' report on Sidney. He closed the folder and leaned forward with his hands under his chin.

She not only had visiting ministers calling her out but now, if the report in front of him was to be believed, it appeared that she was also able to interpret dreams. Sister Damaris confirmed her report verbally.

"She's amazing Pastor Styles. I told her this dream I had the other night and she knew what it meant right off the bat."

"Is that so?"

"Yes. I think you should just hire her."

"What?"

"For the staff position that you're checking her out for."

"Oh yes, that. Well, I don't want to jump the gun too quickly. I still need to make certain that she's living an honorable lifestyle."

"Take it from me. She is walking the walk. She's very, very dedicated. And she's quick to speak up when something doesn't line up with the bible. She sounds like she'd be perfect for a church staff position."

"Yes, well, like I said I'm taking all of this under consideration. Thank you for your time Sister Damaris."

"You're welcome and pastor, there is one more thing I kind of wanted to talk to you about."

"Yes Damaris, what is it?" He was hoping she had seen Sidney participate in something questionable, however slight so that he could use it against her."

"Well, I think I may have been called to the ministry."

Canaan was shocked into silence. "What did you just say?"

"I said I think I may have been called to the ministry and..."

He became more agitated as the girl talked. "I see and does this have anything to do with the dream Sister Lyons interpreted for you the other night?"

"Oh, goodness no! That was a personal issue. I just believe that God is calling me to the ministry. I haven't even told Sidney yet. Anyway, what I'm doing, spying on her, I'm starting to feel guilty about it. I feel like I shouldn't be doing this."

"I see. Well if you have another job lined up then you should take it."

His words were like a bucket of cold water and as he knew she would, she suddenly transformed back into the needy young woman who had first entered his office months ago.

"I mean, I don't have a job, I just wanted to tell you what I felt God was sharing with me."

"That's nice, really. Thanks for sharing. Now if you'll excuse me. I have other matters to attend to." Canaan swiveled his office chair around to put the latest folder in the drawer of the file cabinet where he kept everything related to Sidney. With that gesture Damaris had been dismissed and she took the hint. She got up quickly and walked out the office without a word.

Canaan huffed and puffed as he stood behind his desk. *The least she could have done was close the door.* He felt his ire rise again the more he thought about it. What is the world coming to? *Now the peanut gallery believes they are called to preach the gospel. What next?* He was so sick and tired of these young women popping up with a 'word from the Lord'. All they were doing was distracting the men in the ministry.

Canaan sighed as he picked up the phone. This was nothing more than a wrinkle he would have to straighten out. His oldest son picked up on the third ring.

"Swing by the church on your way home. I need you to do something for me."

"OK Dad."

When Logan arrived, Edna-Jean waved him right into his father's office. Canaan didn't waste any time once the young man sat down.

"You know Damaris Buffet don't you?" Canaan looked up briefly from the book spread open on his desk to eye his son.

"Yeah why?"

"Because she's getting ahead of herself and I need to bring her down a notch."

"What do you want me to do?"

"Find something, any dirty laundry I can use to entice her to keep her mouth shut."

"Okay but Pop, she's a pretty straight arrow. What if I don't find anything?"

Canaan looked at his son out of pure exasperation. "Then you'll create something."

Logan thought about the attractive, older woman and the exact situation he wanted to 'create' with her. "Sure Pop, no problem."

That took care of that little issue. When Logan left he shook his head once again. How was the church going to be what it needed to be when the men wouldn't step up to the plate. Where were the young men who were being called into the ministry? *Now, that Dirk Winston would make a good minister.* He made a mental note to talk to the young man about it next time they spoke.

When his son left, Canaan pulled out the photo of Sidney once more. He knew the photo by heart now, had memorized every detail of the body spread out before the lens of the camera. In his mind he was becoming more attached to Sidney. He even saw her when she wasn't there. He knew the photo had everything to do with his line of thinking but he couldn't bring himself to destroy it. In fact, he hadn't even realized that he now needed to look at it at least three times a day and God help the first person he came across before getting his fix.

He sighed as he replaced the photo. *It will all be over soon.*

***

When Sidney arrived early for bible study on Wednesday evening she felt like something wasn't right. The sleep she experienced the night before had been restless and distressing. She had been on edge for some time now but the uneasiness was growing increasingly worse. She looked around at the crowd that had gathered in the church and everything seemed normal but she still felt something was askew. She tried to join in with everyone else as they sang praise songs but it didn't sooth the building apprehension.

The music died down and then it happened. She sensed it more than saw it, a sudden shift in the atmosphere. The air seemed to condense and grow heavier and could almost be described as stifling. As Pastor Styles and his sons entered the pulpit she grew numb. The word 'deceived' scrolled across her mind as she looked at them. She was happy to know that all eyes were directed toward the front of the church because she couldn't have changed her facial expression if she wanted to. When the pastor bowed his head and announced it was time to pray she did just that.

The benediction was pronounced two hours later and Sidney again rushed out of the sanctuary. She felt like she needed to go somewhere and pray. She tried to pray while she was in the church but it felt like something was blocking her efforts. Once she was in the car she felt better. She immediately started praying for the pastor and his family. She wasn't sure what she had just experienced back there but she knew it wasn't good. She didn't stop praying until she reached home.

Once inside the house she noticed that Meena had retired early and since her little encounter earlier had left her drained, she decided to do the same. She stopped in her home office on her way to the bedroom. When she turned on her computer to check her email it didn't pop up like it usually did. She clicked on the welcome screen and it asked for a password. Still trying to figure out what was going on, she entered her password and was presented with an error message stating that she had used the wrong password.

"What in the world..." She tried the password again, typing more slowly this time to make sure she had entered it correctly. When she got the same message she just shook her head and turned the computer off. She wasn't up for a fight tonight. She would call the internet service provider in the morning.

***

Damaris picked up the ringing phone while she was stretched out on her bed. She had hoped he would call tonight. He approached her as soon as bible study was over to tell her she looked nice. She chatted with him a few more minutes before he asked for her phone number. She would never admit it but she almost broke the sound barrier to get home.

She tried to sound calm when she spoke "Hello?"

"Um, hi. Can I speak to Sister Damaris Buffett please?"

"Speaking. Hi Brother Logan."

"You don't have to put 'brother' in front of my name. Logan is fine."

"Alright. Hi Logan."

"Hi." He paused to let her finish giggling. "You looked great tonight by the way."

"Uh thanks. You mentioned that earlier."

"Oh, I guess I did. It's just that you looked extra special."

"Wow, you give great compliments."

"Well I meant every word. So... what are you wearing right now?"

***

The bedside clock read 03:33 and Sidney had been tossing and turning all night, even after an extended prayer time. She wasn't asleep, not exactly. She was in that in between place but she felt like she was starting to slip away. Her eyes were closed but she unexpectedly saw Canaan Styles clear as day. She saw a gun in his hand, saw him raise his arm and point the gun at her then watched as he seemed to pull the trigger in slow motion. She sprang straight up in a cold sweat with a sob on her lips.

Pray for Him

She was still half asleep and trying to make sense of what she had just seen but she knew the voice of God when she heard it.

"Let me get this straight God, The pastor of the church that I currently attend is trying to kill me and you want me to pray for him."

He's overtaken.

"That's unfortunate." Those were the last words she spoke before she rolled over and went to sleep. It was a fitful sleep but she slept. That little vision she'd seen, as disturbing as it was brought some sense of closure. At least she knew what was going on.

Four short hours later the sun was just beginning to peek through the curtains when the soft voice interrupted the morning.

"Good morning Sidney. You've made it to another day and that means God has something else for you to accomplish. You have been called and chosen by the Most High and that is no light thing. The enemy has already been alerted to your status and is ready to do anything he deems necessary to stop your progress. Prepare yourself because he will use every one of your co-workers, friends, family members and acquaintances that he can. He will also use every situation at his disposal to accomplish this mission against you. Put your trust in the Lord and remember that everyone who smiles at you is not happy for you. Know that everyone who sings your praise in public is not doing the same thing behind closed doors. Gird yourself and know that your God, which began a good work in you, will complete it to the end. Now rise and shine and give God the glory due His name!"

Her mentor, Pastor Esther Cyrus had made that recording for her several months ago and Sidney had been using it as her alarm of choice recently. However, it seemed to have taken on new significance this morning. The pastor attended the same church that her sister Sidra had grown up in. Sidra introduced them several years earlier when Sidney first accepted Christ into her life. Both Pastor Cyrus and Sidney had shown a similarity in spiritual gifts and Pastor Cyrus offered the younger woman guidance whenever she needed it.

Sidney looked at the alarm clock and thought about throwing it into the wall. The calmly spoken words sounded so full of hope and assurance, none of which she felt right now. It didn't seem fair that she should have to see what she saw last night and then turn around and give God anything, much less glory. She slowly turned her face toward the wall and wiped the tears falling down her cheeks. Today felt like a good day to stay in bed.

***

Sidra snuggled against Jensen trying for dear life to hold on to the last quiet part of her day. She knew she would hear cries of hunger at any moment now. When she finally opened her eyes she looked up and saw her husband smiling down at her.

"Good morning wife."

"Good morning husband." She did one final combination of a yawn and stretch before she sat up. "Why are you so happy this morning?"

"Because I have the best wife on the planet."

Sidra grinned like she had just gotten away with something. "Yeah, I outdid myself last night didn't I?"

Jensen laughed and pulled her close. "You absolutely did but I wasn't referring to last night."

"Then to what were you referring?"

"Just life in general. You are the perfect compliment to my life and I'm just happy you allowed me to share in yours."

She kissed his bare chest before giving him a squeeze. "It is my pleasure. And while we're passing out compliments, I want to thank you for being an amazing husband. I honestly wasn't sure how I was going to handle the whole 'submission thing', but thank you for making it easy."

"Yeah, you had me worried too."

She punched him hard in the arm before he had a chance to finish. "Oww! I was going to say but you're doing a great job."

"Mmhmm, I bet you were."

He laughed again. "I was."

"Have you heard anything else about your call to the ministry?

Jensen shook his head. "No. He was pretty clear when he spoke the first time but I asked him for a sign to confirm it anyway."

"If He was so clear, why ask for a sign?" She propped herself up on one elbow to wait for his answer.

"Scared I guess? This is a huge step, not just for us but for the kids as well."

"I know and if it was really God you heard, we are all in this together. Where you go, I'll follow. But God knows that we want to wait for Him to send us confirmation. I believe He will when the time is right."

"Yeah, you're right as usual. Now let me ask you, why are your kids so quiet this morning?"

Sidra hopped up and ran out the door. "Oh, I forgot to check on them."

When she ran past Kyra's room the door was open and the bed was empty. She stopped at the twins' room next and couldn't believe her eyes. They were both in their cribs quietly drinking their bottles and listening to Kyra read them a story. They were three perfect little angels.

"Kyra?"

Upon hearing her name the little girl looked up and smiled. "I heard you and Daddy talking so I figured I'd fix their bottles and keep them quiet for a little bit. That was ok to do right?"

Sidra was overwhelmed. "Sweetie that was more than ok. You have just earned yourself pizza for dinner tonight."

Kyra jumped straight up and yelled "Whoo hoo!" so loudly that she scared both babies into dropping their bottles. Of course they screamed like someone was chasing them. Sidra just shook her head. Two babies crying and one fourth grader jumping around and yelling, now that was the noise she was used to in the mornings.

***

When Saturday morning rolled around Sidney sauntered down to the kitchen to make breakfast. As she was cracking the eggs into a bowl, she heard it again.

Pray for Him.

She slung some pots around, almost knocked the refrigerator over and managed to turn the stove on without burning the house down but after several minutes she was able to force "God help him" out of her mouth in the midst of her inner turmoil. She said it but she couldn't leave it alone.

"God, I don't understand."

He's overtaken.

"I still don't understand. What's that got to do with me? And why not ask someone he's not trying to kill to pray for him?"

He's opened a door. Pray for those around him.

113

"But why me?"

There was no answer to that final question. She ate her breakfast and went through the entire day pondering recent events. She hadn't seen Pastor Cyrus in several months. Maybe her mentor would be able to help her make some sense of this. Meena wandered into the kitchen just as Sidney was finishing her breakfast.

"You're going to the 11:00 service in the morning aren't you?" her aunt wanted to know.

"Um, no. But I can drop you off and then swing back by to pick you up when it's over."

"Oh? You have other plans?"

"Yeah, I'm going to visit a friend's church."

The thought had just popped into her head but given the circumstances she wouldn't feel comfortable going to Hearts Desire any longer. And it wasn't a lie. She had plenty of friends who had asked her to visit their church over the last few years. She usually declined because she was too busy at her own church but she would pick one tomorrow and go.

The next morning, after dropping Meena off, Sidney met her friend Aarelyn at a small church about twenty minutes away from her house. The choir was wonderful and the preacher was even better but most importantly, the atmosphere felt right. She felt like she could breathe freely there and she did. She enjoyed the service and told her host as much.

"Thanks girl, I had a great time."

Aarelyn smiled at her friend. "I'm glad you finally made it. I'll have to make time to get over to your church too, it's just that I'm so busy here."

Sidney smiled back, thinking something entirely different than what came out of her mouth. "Oh trust me I understand. Seems like there's always something going on."

"You can say that again. Oh that reminds me. Walk over to this table with me. I told someone I would sign up to help at the Health Expo."

Sidney vaguely recalled hearing an announcement on the radio about it. "Oh right. That starts next week doesn't it?"

"Yes, and my friend said they still need help. If you have some free time, you should think about signing up."

I have nothing but free time. "You know, I think I will. Sounds like it might be fun."
***

How dare she! Canaan paced back and forth in his church office. He had actually spent time writing out a sermon to deliver to his congregation and she wasn't there. And worse, she had the nerve to attend someone else's church this morning. He sat back down at his desk and fumed at the screen. The GPS locator showed her car parked in a town about thirty minutes away. When he pulled the address up on the internet search engine he saw that it was a church belonging to a pastor he met a couple of times at functions around town. *Well, if she thinks she can get away from me that easily, she's got another think coming. I've got eyes everywhere.*

He picked up the phone and dialed the number he'd just copied down from the computer screen. "Yes, hello? Pastor Lansing? Hi, how are you? This is Pastor Canaan Styles. We met at a church function last year... Yes, that's the one.... Oh I'm fine. Thanks for asking. Listen, I don't want to take up too much of your time but the reason I'm calling is because you had a visitor this morning, a young woman by the name of Sidney Lyons... Right, and... well I don't normally do things like this, but we men of God and particularly pastors have to stick together." He waited calmly for the other man to agree with him. "I just want you to be careful with that particular woman. I don't know why she was at your church this morning but she's been going here for a while and all I will say is you would want to keep an eye on her when she's there...Yes un-huh, I know, they all seem normal at first..."

***

Damaris rolled over and looked at the handsome man lying asleep next to her. It had been exactly ten days since their first phone conversation but they talked every day for several hours so she felt like she knew him well. He had thoroughly rocked her world last night and she just couldn't believe her luck. First God had called her into the ministry and now this man, a minister and the pastor's son said he loved her. The word marriage

116

had even come up. She didn't even mind the ten-year difference between their ages. Her future was on the right track. She could just feel it. She was so lost in thought that she didn't notice him staring at her.

"Good morning beautiful."

"Good morning Logan." She cuddled next to him enjoying the feel of his body. *Mrs. Logan Styles, I like the way that sounds.*

"So what do you have planned today?" he wanted to know.

"I have a meeting at the church later but that's about it. What's on your agenda for the day?"

"You ...and then I'll figure the rest out as I go along."

"You are insatiable." She smiled as she said it to let him know she didn't mind one bit.

"Well if you'd gotten home earlier last night we could have gotten started sooner. What took you so long anyway?"

"You know the traffic is always bad on the beltway on Friday nights."

He nodded. "Oh, where were you coming from?"

"Church"

"What in the world was going on at church on Friday evening?"

"I had to meet with your father about some things."

That piqued his interest. "What kind of things."

She shrugged nonchalantly. "Just stuff."

He pulled her close and gave her a squeeze. "Hey, I thought we told each other everything."

She still wasn't sure she should say anything. After all, the pastor had sworn her to secrecy but she had just made love to this man and was planning on doing it again in the very near future, it seemed silly to hold a simple thing like this back from him.

"Your dad asked me to keep an eye on Sidney Lyons."

He sat straight up. "Did he now?" Logan had the same opinion of his father as his brother Conner but took the long absences in stride, probably because he knew that one day he would be expected to take over as head of the church. He did agree with Conner on one point though, and that was Mrs. Styles, his mother was to be protected at all costs.

Damaris was oblivious to his chain of thought and kept talking. "Yeah, he said he was considering her for a position on staff but he needed to make sure she was living a good Christian walk."

"And you believed him?"

"You don't?"

"Baby, there is only one reason I would ever have to check up on a woman like that..."

She gasped when her mind suddenly filed in the blank. "They're having an affair?"

He shook his head in unbelief. "You know when my brother told me what he'd found, I didn't believe him but I do now."

"What did he find?"

"Nude pictures, some nasty emails and a GPS tracker on her car."

"That little sleaze. She walks around here so pious like she's never done anything wrong and here she is sleeping around, and with the pastor of all people. What should we do?"

"I think my brother's already got it figured out. We can just join his party, the destroy Sidney Lyons party."

She sat up and shifted herself toward the edge of the bed. "Right!"

He grabbed her arm and pulled her back down. "Wait."

"What's wrong?"

"I have an itch I need scratched awfully bad."

She smiled at the virile young man. "I can take care of that for you."

***

It was late and Sidney was in her car just leaving the Convention Center in Downtown Washington, D.C. She had volunteered herself for both weeks that the health expo was going on thinking it would give her time away from church to think. That she needed to find a new church was apparent to her but where she could go that she wouldn't be followed was now the question. It was more than obvious by now what was going. If she had any doubt, the pastor from Aarelyn's church cleared it up for her.

When she arrived at the small church earlier this week to pick up her schedule for the health expo, the pastor came out of his office and just stared at her. The look on his face landed somewhere between pity and disgust. He never took his eyes off of her, almost like he was watching her to make sure she didn't shoplift any items or kidnap any children from the church. She looked back at the man with her own brand of pity. Between the strange occurrences and the directives from God, she'd had some time to process what was happening. However, she couldn't get over how easily so many people accepted a lie as the truth. It made her wonder how often she had done it in her own life.

Oh well she thought. *From the looks of things, this will all be over soon.* Sidney glanced up into her rear view mirror five minutes after exiting onto the highway and noticed the small dark car about 60 yards behind her in the lane to her right. She only had to shift in her seat slightly to see that there was another vehicle, an SUV about 40 yards behind the other car in the far left lane. *Hmm. I wonder if the hunter has realized that he's become the hunted? Probably not.* She reached for the radio and turned up the volume as she sang along with the song that was playing. She lifted her voice in sweet harmony with *Fred Hammond*, "No weapon formed against me shall prosper. It won't work…"

Quis custodiet ipsos custodes? (Who watches the watchmen?) ~Juvenal

CHAPTER 7

"Pastor Cyrus, there are some days I wake up and actually think I'm losing my mind or I've already gone crazy."

Sidney decided to talk to someone before she exploded. She could have gone to her sister but she knew she needed proof before anything could be done. Pastor Cyrus was the only other alternative and it turned out, the best alternative for this situation.

The older woman shook her head as she poured two cups of Earl Grey tea. "Baby, I know this can't be easy for you but God isn't giving you information to make you crazy. He's trying to help you."

"Help me? By letting it continue? How is that helping me? I'm actually trying to live for God and I have to put up with this foolishness from so called Christians! Why He doesn't just kill them I don't know, and believe me I asked."

"And how's that working out for you?"

"They woke up this morning just like I did."

"You mean God caused the sun to shine on the just and the unjust today? Wow, that is news."

"So it wasn't one of my more stellar prayers but I am just so angry!"

"Sidney, child this may be hard to accept right now, but God loves them as much as He loves you. They are His children too. They are wayward children but He loves them enough to give them time to repent. He's not going to throw them away over a mistake."

Sidney sank back into the office chair. "A mistake makes it sound so trivial, like they don't know what they're doing. Like some kind of way they couldn't help it."

Pastor Cyrus covered Sidney's hand with her own weathered hand. "Listen to me." She waited several moments until the younger woman looked up and met her eyes. "I am in no way condoning what is going on because God has given us power over the enemy and we have the power to say no and walk away..."

Sidney's voice was barely audible when she spoke "but?"

Pastor Cyrus nodded. "But when you reach a certain level of influence in the kingdom, you are rewarded by the enemy with very powerful demons whose constant goal is to bring you down and along with you, any weak Christians who were more entranced with an idol or a mindset than with God."

Sidney already knew the answer but she asked anyway. "Even if that idol is a leader in the church?"

"I'm afraid so." Pastor Cyrus had grabbed her own cup of tea by then and was leaning back into the small sofa. Something about the tone of her voice made Sidney look closer.

The dawning of realization suddenly lighted and Sidney slid to the edge of her chair so she could be closer to the other woman. "You're speaking from experience, aren't you? You can talk me through this because you've already been down this road."

"Esther Cyrus, you are nobody's prophet!" She had traveled back in time to some unknown place and Sidney sat still, afraid she wouldn't continue if interrupted. Esther's eyes had a far-away look but the pain was evident and easily called up. "That's what the group of preachers told me. They had all been preaching for over twenty years, had seen thousands come to the Lord for salvation but none had ever managed to have a dream or vision that foretold the future. They didn't know what to make of me. Back then, God just didn't give gifts like that to young women." She smiled ruefully. "Or if He did, none of them ever came forward." Young women were supposed to settle down and push out a few babies, not proclaim the future and, especially not with any authority from the Lord. " One tear slowly formed and ran down the soft brown cheek. "Eventually, they ran me out of town by telling everyone I was involved in witchcraft."

Sidney was boiling. She hopped to her feet and paced back and forth in the small office. "So this is what I have to look forward to? Men who are jealous of a God-given gift pushing me away because they don't understand it?' A shrill laugh escaped her throat. "These are the same men who are supposed to be helping me! Well fine! If they want me gone, then...."

"Careful..."

Sidney let out a controlled scream. "Ahhhhh! It's just not right! It's not fair that God let's this kind of thing go on!"

Pastor Cyrus came and stood with her. She grabbed the warm mug out of Sidney's hands and carefully placed it on the desk. "What does Romans 8:28 say?"

Sidney was so upset that she didn't answer for a moment. She finally pushed the words out with a forcefulness that surprised even her. "That all things work together for the good of those that love God...and... it's not right." She managed the last few words through her tears.

"And to those that are the called, according to His purpose. Honey, I told you before, being called is a serious thing and for the record, being pushed out of that little hick town is the best thing that ever happened to me."

Another light bulb went off for Sidney and she looked at her friend with new understanding. "If they hadn't pushed you out, you wouldn't be here at this church or even for me."

"Exactly! And besides all of that, this is a battle about authority."

"What do you mean?"

Esther smiled. "God allowed this test for Pastor Styles. He may have failed it but you have a chance to pass it."

Sidney shook her head slowly. "I'm sorry but I still don't understand. Who's authority are we speaking of?"

She grabbed Sidney's hand and walked her to the couch before sitting down. "Yours baby-doll."

The sigh of frustration just couldn't be helped. Sidney stood looking down at the older woman who was quite relaxed now. With a pained expression, she plopped down on the sofa. "Could ya help a sister out?"

One final gulp and the contents of the colorful ceramic vessel had been consumed by the gray-haired woman. "I'd love to sweets but I have a class to teach now." She was at the door in a flash and gave a cryptic grin before she turned the knob. "Let's get together next week. Don't forget to lock the door when you leave, found out last week that one of our co-workers needs to be delivered from a spirit of thievery. Oh, and remember there is a friend who..."

"Sticks closer than a brother, yeah, yeah" Sidney watched the door close behind Pastor Cyrus and suddenly she was all alone. She still had no idea what the last half of the conversation had been about and the little office was offering up not one clue so she decided to move on.

When she reached the foyer she heard her name being called.

"Sid?"

She was more than a little surprised because she had only been to the church a handful of times in the past few years. When the man caught up with her he stopped about two feet away.

"Oh, you're not Sidra."

Sidney smiled. "Afraid not" She had almost forgotten that Sidra grew up in this church. Now she attended Jensen's church.

"You must be her sister then."

"That I am."

"Wow, you two really could pass for twins. How is she doing anyway?"

"Oh, she and her family are great. I spoke to them the other night."

"Great, tell her McCoy family said hello."

"I sure will."

Sidney got back in her car and pulled out of the parking lot. She really had thought about telling Sidra and Jensen but the same thing stopped her again and again. She had no proof and she knew they would need that before doing anything about her problem.

She didn't want to go home, not just yet so she drove around for a little while and before she knew it she was headed to the small diner near her house that she had become fond of. She wasn't surprised to see Officer Winston walk in shortly after she did. *Really God? The devil gets to hunt me down in the name of Jesus and everybody, including you, says nothing about it?* She finished her meal quickly and headed home knowing that not one but two vehicles were following her.

***

Damaris logged into Sidney's Facebook account for the umpteenth time as Sidney. She and both the Styles brothers had been doing it for months now. It was like second nature to her. The very first time Sidney changed her password and Damaris couldn't get into the account, she was forced to go to Pastor Styles. After that he just told her how to hack into the account on her own and there was nothing Sidney could do about it. It didn't matter what she changed the password to, when she logged back on to the internet, Damaris would be able to hack into the account with the equipment Pastor Styles had given her.

When Damaris looked at the account today, she decided that Sidney had too many friends. She usually dealt with this in one of two ways. Either she just deleted some friends or she sent out an email to the friends she targeted that day. The email would look like it was from Sidney and be so obnoxious and morally bankrupt that the friend would either block Sidney or end the electronic friendship altogether. Since she had time, she did both.

She then hacked into Sidney's email accounts and deleted any messages that would benefit Sidney in any way because according to Damaris and the two Styles children, Sidney didn't deserve anything good in her life. She knew Conner did the same thing every few days also. They had even managed to score some stuff Sidney had won online. Of course Sidney never received the email. They just picked up the prizes for her. It's not that she enjoyed stealing from Sidney but Damaris reasoned that someone had to show her she couldn't pretend to be one way in church and live a completely different way outside of church. She remembered something Logan had said as he rolled out of bed the other day.

"Sounds like more than one of the visiting ministers think she's anointed. That's the word around the church anyway."

Damaris continued to hit the delete key. Sidney had been slow in returning her calls the last few days anyway. If Sidney didn't want her as a friend, she didn't need to make any new ones. The more she thought about it, the madder she got. She was just as anointed as Sidney Lyons. It wasn't fair that she got all the attention because she was the Pastor's favorite. All she was doing was trying to even the playing field a little.

***

The tired man looked around his office at the stacks of paperwork piled up on his desk and credenza. His heart broke a little every time he looked at those stacks because he knew each one represented some evil doing or some wicked person who had hurt someone else just to get a step ahead or to fulfill some perverted craving. He wondered how it was the people perpetrating these crimes never seemed to realize they would eventually end up back where they started or worse. He also wondered if the God his family constantly spoke about was actually real. *What kind of God allows these types of degenerate acts to happen to innocent people, many of them children?* He was about ready to shut down his computer and head home when he heard the sharp rap at his door.

"Come in."

The younger man poked his head in the door and scanned the room to make sure they were alone. Once he was certain, he closed the door behind him and handed a manila folder across the desk. "We've been working on this case for a while but I thought you might find it interesting." He was back at the door and ready to leave as quickly as he'd come but turned to give one final piece of information. "Agent West, our team was told to start focusing on the top dog but there are a few pups who need to be collared before they get out of hand and it's getting pretty bad pretty fast. If it was my family, I'd want to know." His closing words vaguely explained the purpose of the folder but not the contents. The young man closed the door behind him and headed toward the elevator at the end of the hallway.

Justice stared down at the unmarked folder for a moment before opening it. Something in his gut didn't feel right and he knew before he opened the file that he was not going to like what he saw. A picture was stapled to the top sheet of paper and his heart stopped when he saw it. "What the hell..." He flipped frantically through the rest of file, speed-reading as he went.

Ten minutes later he had read the file twice and was still unable to move. Justice had seen plenty of injustice during his years as a federal agent but this had to take the cake. In fact, it seemed that the evil forces in the world had ramped up considerably over the last few years and he wondered what in the world could be going on. He wasn't into the whole religious thing like the rest of his family but he had met enough devils in his line of work to know one when he saw it and this depravity was straight out of hell.

His office phone rang and momentarily wiped away thoughts of the folder when he saw the number on the caller-id. "Hey big bro, I was just thinking about you."

Jensen laughed. "You were huh? Not enough to call though."

Justice smiled. Jensen was always getting on him about not staying in touch but with his job, there was no way he could do it, not regularly anyway. This time though he was definitely about to call. "Whatever man, I was two seconds from picking up the phone. So, what's going on down there in the DMV?" The D.C. metro area was actually made up of a portion of Maryland and Virginia along with D.C. so most of the locals and residents had taken to calling it 'the DMV.'

"All is well man. Your niece wanted to holler at you right quick. How are things in Texas?"

"Hot. Get my baby on the phone"

Jensen laughed. "I'll bet. Hold on, she's coming."

Justice's heart warmed up instantly and he started grinning from ear to ear. He laughed at himself before Kyra got on the line. Anyone hearing him talk about the little girl would have thought he had fathered her instead of Jensen.

"Uncle Just!"

"Hey now! How's one of my most favoritest princesses doing?"

Kyra giggled. "Uncle Just, you know favoritest is not a word."

"Yes it is. If I said it, then it's a word."

"Nah-unh."

"Unh-huh."

They stayed on the phone about ten minutes while Kyra filled him in on the latest happenings in the fourth grade. She was just winding down when he heard Jensen in the background say "Ky, you're not gonna tell you're uncle about your boyfriend?"

"Daddy!" Kyra shrieked into the phone so loudly that Justice had to pull the phone away from his ear but he sat straight up. *Boyfriend...already?*

"Kyra, did your daddy just say you had a boyfriend?"

He could almost see her roll those big brown eyes and put her hands on her imaginary hips before she answered him. "Uncle Just, Tevin is not my boyfriend. He's just a friend from school."

"Mmmhm, that's all it better be. Put your daddy back on the phone."

He heard he suck her teeth and sigh but caught her just before she handed the phone over without saying anything. "Hey."

"Yes?"

"I love you."

Kyra giggled like he was used to before saying "I love you more."

"Nah-unh."

"Unh-huh, hold on here's daddy."

Jensen got back on the phone with a smile on his face because he knew what was coming.

"J. Man, are you serious, boys already?"

"Just, this is the last month of school. Two months from then we enter double digits. A month after that she's headed to fifth grade. The year after that our baby is in middle school."

"Wow, it's been ten years already?

"Afraid so."

Justice shook his head. *Where had the time gone?* "And who is Tevin?"

"This is the first time I'm hearing his name but brother, you better believe I'm all over it."

"Yeah. You, me and a few hundred agents."

Jensen laughed loudly. "Ha-ha! Just, man the boy is only ten. I don't think you need to call out the big guns just yet. Plus, I'm not completely sure what's gone on. I don't hear all the good stuff. Sidra gets all the dirt during their so-called spa days and I get filtered info when they get home."

Hearing Sidra's name reminded him of the folder sitting on his desk. "Speaking of Sidra, how's my favorite sister-in-law doing?"

"Oh she's fine and she's right here. You want to talk to her?"

"Yeah, put pretty woman on the line."

Jensen smiled at his brother's remark but gave him a playful warning all the same. "Hey, watch yourself."

"Hey bro, you picked her. I just call them like I see them."

134

Justice stayed on the phone with Sidra for a few minutes before they wrapped up but just as the conversation was ending he slipped in one last question. "Hey Sidra, how's your sister doing?"

"Oh, she's great. She's been busy volunteering at some health event going on downtown so we haven't seen her in a bit. I think it's only supposed to go on for a couple of weeks though so it should be ending next week."

Bingo. "That's good to hear. Tell her I said Hi next time you talk to her."

"OK, sure will and Justice, please take care of yourself out there."

"I will sis. I promise. Bye."

He hung up the call but had the handset back in his hand quickly. After waiting through several rings, the other person finally picked up.

Justice twisted his neck to stretch out the kinks before talking. "Hey man, you're in home in DC for a while aren't you?"

"J.W.? Yeah, vacationing and bored out of my mind though, why what's going on?"

"I think my sister-in-law may be in some kind of trouble. There's some big health thing going on downtown right?"

Terrence scratched his head for a moment. "Oh yeah, the national health expo. They're at the convention center for a couple weeks. What do you need?"

Justice sent up a silent *thank you* for solid friends and favors owed. "I need to call in a favor."

"Whatever man, you've saved my behind enough times that you don't have to ask anymore. What's up?"

He ended the call with Terrence 30 minutes later and scanned the folder once more before leaving his office for the night. Justice grabbed his gym bag out the corner of his office and headed down to the fitness center in the basement of building. He had some serious stress to work off. At first glance he thought the picture staring back at him was of Sidra. She and her sister look so much alike but it didn't matter which sister it was. Family was family and he was in the business of protecting people, especially family. He shook his head once more. There may not be enough time to work off what he was feeling tonight. Wicked drug dealers and serial killers were one thing. Wicked preachers were something he just couldn't wrap his head around.

***

Canaan left the young engaged couple he had just performed pre-marital counseling with in a classroom and headed back to his office. Vern, the church custodian was in the hallway as usual. Canaan would swear that Vern cleaned the same spot in front of the restrooms thirty times a day to catch everything that was happening in the church.

The older man spoke first. "How's it going pastor?"

"Alright Vernon, and how about with you?"

"Fair to middling I suppose. Hey have you seen Sister Lyons around?"

Vern didn't know it but he struck a nerve.

"Uh, I'm not sure who you mean." Canaan had become so practiced in lying that he was sure his remark sounded sincere.

Vern wasn't fazed. "You know, Sidney Lyons, real pretty girl with the shoulder length hair."

"Oh yes, I know who you're talking about now." Canaan had been wondering the same thing in all actuality but after he received Damaris' report regarding the health expo he confirmed it when he tracked her car online to the convention center. He did it every evening now but tonight was Wednesday and he was sure she would skip the event downtown and come to church tonight.

"I didn't realize you knew her." The words rushed out so quickly but Canaan stopped himself from saying anything else. If someone didn't know any better, they might get the impression that he was jealous.

"Oh, I don't, not well anyway but I know when the hand of God is on someone. I just miss seeing her light around here, that's all."

"What do you mean her light?"

He looked at the pastor strangely. "I mean, you know, her aura."

"Aura?" *More of the peanut gallery hearing from God again?*

"Right, the saints with the gift of second sight always have a different aura but then, I suppose I'm the only one that sees it. My mother used to warn me about saying things like that to people. Forget I said anything."

The man had Canaan's attention now. "No, no, go on Vern, I understand. You say she has the gift of second sight?"

The old man was nodding vigorously now, happy that he could share his own gift with someone. "Almost sure of it. That one sees things coming before they get to her. I'm not sure how but some kind of way God speaks to certain people like that, you know tells 'em things before they actually happen. And she's one of 'em. I can tell it by her light."

Canaan reached out and patted the man on the shoulder. "Thank you Vern, this conversation has been very enlightening."

Canaan rushed down the hall to his office so he could process this new piece of information. *I wonder if she knows anything about what I've been doing*? He gathered his notes for the service that would happen later that night as he reviewed the conversation with Vern in his mind. *Probably not* he mused to himself. *That 'second sight' stuff is probably a bunch of bunk anyway.*

We must not be deceived into believing we can do as we please, live contrary to God's laws, and still be welcome before our Father, let alone move in significant intercessory authority for others... God unquestionably links our authority level to our purity level.

~ Dutch Sheets

CHAPTER 8

The next day a stealthy figure made it's way through the large parking deck without drawing any attention. But then, it was dusk and he was used to doing that. He paused and smiled thinking about the nickname his co-workers had dubbed him, 'shinobi,' the ninja. Everyone in his office knew that if something needed to be done quickly and covertly Terrence was the man to call. They had no idea though how he'd come to posses those traits.

No one knew that after graduating college Terrence decided to spend one year touring the world. Twelve amazing months later his trip had ended and he was less than twenty-four hours away from heading back to the Tokyo airport for a U.S.

bound flight. On a whim he decided to do some sightseeing in the countryside before leaving the beautiful nation.

He'd been gone for most of the day when he traveled off the main path and found himself in the middle of a small village. One young boy was happy to show him the way back to the main road but on their way stopped by the hut of the village elder. Terrence was astonished to learn that the old man had just turned ninety years old because he moved like a man of thirty. The little boy informed Terrence that the old man was one of the last remaining ninjas and that he would teach anyone who wanted to learn the ways of a true ninja. Terrence spent three more years in that little village before the old man died of natural causes. He made an oath on the old man's deathbed that he would not divulge the location of the village or the full extent of what he had learned. The nickname he picked up since his return was a happy coincidence but Terrence never confirmed nor denied anything about his past. He would always say, "I was shown a few moves". When he returned to the states he was quickly recruited by the FBI and had been there ever since.

He found Sidney's car with no problem from the description and tag number Justice had texted him earlier. He made sure no one was around when he leaned against the car and slowly lowered himself to the ground. It took him less than a minute to locate the small tracking device that had been placed under Sidney's car. He knew it was secured with a magnet and without her knowledge. When the device was removed he texted the make and serial number to Justice so they could track it also. Next, he placed it underneath the car next to hers with out-of-state tags. *Let them chase that rabbit for a while.* When he stood up, he checked once more to make sure he didn't have any company then he made his way into the convention center.

Justice had told him that Sidney was working as a volunteer at the health fair with the national urban league. He spotted Sidney at the organization's booth shortly after he walked in but he walked around to the all of the other exhibits so as not to arouse suspicion. More than twenty minutes had passed before he made his way over to Sidney and struck up a conversation.

He read her nametag as he approached the booth. "Hi, how are you Sidney?"

Sidney smiled at the attractive guy. His olive skin and Asian features under a mass of dark curly hair gave him an almost exotic appearance. She had almost gotten used to complete strangers walking up and calling her by name but not quite. "I'm good, thanks. Did you get registered for your free health screening?"

"Um, yeah just a few minutes ago as a matter of fact."

She reached under the table to bring up more brochures and handed him two. "Good, here's more info on prostate exams and colon health. It's important to take care of yourself."

The face he made after she said 'prostate exam' caused her to laugh and take a closer look at her visitor. When they locked eyes the word 'protector' immediately flashed across her mind.

She broke eye contact a second later. *This should be interesting.*

Terrence stayed at the table talking with her for about ten minutes before he asked her out. "Would you like to go get some coffee?" Ordinarily she would have said 'no' without thinking about it but after the stamp of approval she'd seen a few minutes ago, one she assumed was from God, she figured she might as well give her consent.

"I'm not much of a coffee drinker but I could have a cup of tea."

He laughed. "Actually, you could have more than that since it's a little late. You have a taste for anything special?"

She smiled as she remembered passing one of her favorite restaurants on the way in this morning. "Now that you mention it, I've been wanting a burger for the last week."

"I'm always up for a burger. There's a little place called Busboys and Poets not too far from here."

Sidney's smile got broader. "I know it's one of my favorites. How about I meet you there in an hour?"

"That will work."

While Sidney waited for the stragglers to work their way around to her booth before the event shut down for the evening, Terrence went and moved his car closer to Sidney's and waited. From the way Justice described the situation yesterday, he'd do well to keep an eye out on Sidney whenever he was able. He would follow at a safe distance so she wouldn't see him on the way to the restaurant. While waiting, he noticed the car that he had placed the tracking device on back out and head for the garage exit. He wondered what Sidney's stalkers would do when the car reached Maine.

***

Several hours later Canaan turned off the lights in the sanctuary and headed for his office. Bible study had gone well tonight but he was so sure Sidney was going to be there. She'd been absent the last couple of Sundays also. God only knows what type of people she was running in to downtown. What if her gift of second sight had kicked in and convinced her that she didn't need to belong to his church any more.

He had to do something to gain control of the situation. He'd already started bringing in others to help him watch her. He was starting to receive more recognition since he'd started telling the visiting men of God that he was taking an interest in Sidney. It seemed now that almost every visitor who saw her pointed out the young woman, so there was no lack of opportunity. Canaan reasoned that they didn't have to know exactly what he meant by 'taking an interest' in Sidney. He was handling the situation as he saw fit and God hadn't said otherwise.

But things were quickly getting out of hand. There was no way he would be able to keep Sidney isolated from others for much longer. Monitoring her cell phone and email was definitely helping but wouldn't work forever. Was there no way to get her alone and make her understand that he was the only one who could lead her and guide her like she needed? He may have been wrong in the beginning but he saw everything clearly now. He had studied her for these long months. He could now see what the others saw. Only he knew that he was the only one with real insight. He was the only one who had come to care for her as much as any man could and he was the only man on the planet that would be able to get her to the next level that God intended for her.

He rubbed his forehead in frustration. There was no earthly way he could think of that would make her understand what was going on. That he needed to be close to her in order to help her.

The cost of needing to be near her at all times, however, was taking its' toll. It was draining him mentally and physically.

He had gotten to the point where he needed to see what she had on and how she put it on. He wanted to know what she doing every minute of the day. It was becoming too much for him. He didn't know how he could go on at this pace much longer. Having her that far away was driving him crazy.

You could take her.

The voice sounded so close to Canaan's ear that he literally jumped out of his chair. "Who said that?" Spinning around on the swiveled cushion confirmed that he was the only man in the room. *But I heard it.* He got up and looked all around the stately office as if someone could actually hide in plain sight. Deciding that he had over-worked himself for the day, he gathered his belongings and headed toward home. He never did see the demon lounging in the corner... or see it walk out with him to catch a ride in his front seat ...but he heard it all the way home.

He had almost reached his house, was two turns away in fact, when the familiar tug began to pull at his heart. He *needed* to see her again. He had to see her several times a day now because the picture wasn't enough. He needed Sidney like a drowning man needs air. His mind raced around in circles until the realization dawned on him. "God help me. I'm in love." He was in love with another woman other than his wife and he didn't know what to do about it. It was clear to him that the feelings ran deep. He would have to take action of some kind, but what? Should he tell Sidney or should he just divorce his wife and then pursue her?

What if she was the one you were supposed to be with all along? The voice was right inside his head now and sounding like his own thoughts. *What if you made bad choices to escape your father and married the wrong woman? This charade should not continue. It must be corrected. It must be made right.* Canaan pulled into his driveway and once he reached the front door he made straight for his private office. He didn't even stop to speak to his family. He just closed the office door behind him and sat down in front of the LCD monitor. He turned on the small live cameras that were hidden in Sidney's house but only saw Ms. Meena so he logged onto the world wide web to track the signal from the GPS unit hidden under the body of her car.

When the image finally loaded panic struck him full force. *This can't be right. Something must be wrong. She's right outside New York?*

***

Sidney smiled at the handsome face across the table as they finished their dinner. The long wait in line they endured when they arrived was made easier by his natural charm and easy conversation. They had taken their time and enjoyed dinner but most of the food had disappeared long ago.

Sidney had a far-away look in her eyes. "Oh, Europe sounds wonderful. I've only been to the Caribbean but one day, I'm going to travel the world."

"You should. It's a beautiful planet we live on."

"I know. I'm just afraid I'm going to end up in a foreign land with no way to get around. I'm terrible about picking up other languages."

They talked for several minutes more. He had just made some corny joke about how many Christians it took to screw in a light bulb but Sidney knew the current that flowed under his laugh was serious. She decided to change the subject before addressing it though. "So tell me about your family."

He shrugged. "I never met them so anything I said would be kind of a stretch."

"You're adopted?"

"No, I was never so lucky. I spent all of my childhood in foster care. When I turned thirteen, I was attacked by a group of boys on the way home from school. I fought back and ended up in a group home until I aged out of the system."

"Wow."

"Yeah, but enough about me, I bet you have a wonderful family somewhere that loves you, huh?"

Her face lit up when the image of her family popped into her mind. "I do but I just met them a few years ago."

Terrence was genuinely surprised. "That sounds fascinating. Tell me more."

When Sidney finished her tale he looked at her with new eyes. "That was you all over the news a few years ago in the defense trial with that moron singer Mocha?"

She looked up sheepishly. "Guilty."

His laugh lines became deeper before he flashed a bright smile. "I was glad he got what he deserved but I'd heard you were proven innocent, at least by default."

She nodded, laughing now. "Yes, Jesus loves me. He provided some evidence at the last minute that proved my innocence."

She noticed he didn't say much after that and she knew why. She finished the last drop of liquid in her cup before asking him a question, the answer to which she already knew - a direct question about faith. "So, you're not into the whole religious scene I take it." It was a statement more than a question.

Justice had hipped him to Sidney's newly found belief system on the phone the other day. He wasn't one to begrudge any one anything so he didn't really mind. If she thought religion was something she needed to get through this life then she could have it. He, however, had seen too much. There was too much destruction and pain happening to the weakest and most innocent members of society for there to be a living and caring God in his humble opinion.

"You know convention says you're not supposed to discuss religion and politics with non family members don't you?"

She gave a sly look. "I've never been much for convention and would actually be shocked to hear that you were."

One corner of his mouth tilted upward. "OK, you got me."

"That's what I thought. Now back to my question."

"Look, I just don't think any real God would let some of the stuff going on in the world go on, you know. Why would a God so full of love let so much hate exist? But you probably don't get what I'm saying."

She shook her head knowingly. "That is where you'd be wrong. I understand what you're saying completely and up until a few years ago, I actually felt the same way."

"Let me guess, and then you had some big religious experience where the light shone down and the angelic choir started singing and suddenly you were 'saved' from all your sins."

She shook her head and laughed lightly. "Not exactly. I just had a conversation with God that let me know that He was real. The God I had been guessing and wondering about was actually listening to me and He let me know it."

Terrence looked directly into her eyes. "Conversation like a two-way dialogue or a monologue on your part?"

"Dialogue"

He looked doubtful. "So, you actually heard God speak to you?"

Sidney nodded her affirmation. "Not an audible voice but yeah, I heard Him loud and clear"

Noting her earnestness, he merely leaned back in his chair and settled in for the ride. "Alright, this should be good. Let me hear it."

She doubted he would believe anything she said from that point on but all she could do was tell him the truth and leave the rest up to God. She took her time finding a starting point for the story so she wouldn't throw in any unnecessary information but when she decided on one, she just let it flow.

"It started in the middle of all that mess with Mocha. It was a Tuesday or a Wednesday and I was staying with my sister because I was on house arrest. Anyway, she and the man she was dating then, the one she's married to now, had some type of argument and Sidra hadn't heard from him in a couple of days."

She paused long enough to see if he was following her and he gave her a cursory nod to let her know he was.

"Well, I had kind of been checking out her church's online services for a few weeks by then and there was this one particular song they used to sing that just stuck with me. It would pop in my head at the strangest times. This time it popped up one night before I went to bed. I was still singing when I got into bed."

She paused as the waiter came over to take away their plates and leave the check. Terrence hadn't moved.

"When I got into bed I said something to myself like 'I want to believe in a true God but how can I know if it's real. A voice just kind of broke into my thoughts right then and said 'Try Me'. I started asking questions, lots of them and before I could finish forming the thought, the answer was right there.'"

"What kind of questions and answers?" He still seemed dubious but was a little more open now.

She hesitated. "I don't really remember. Everything was so fast and furious." He had sat up a little straighter waiting to hear her response but at her admission leaned back further in his chair. She saw the look on his face and tried to address it. "Look, I know what you're thinking, and honestly, I was wondering the same thing too, if I was going crazy, so I asked one question at the end that would assure me one way or the other."

He hadn't moved from his reclined position. "What question was that?"

"I asked if Jensen was alive and if so, where was he."

"Well, since you said they're married now, I'm guessing the answer to the first part of the question was yes? So what was the rest of the answer?" There was no need to tell her that he'd known Jensen for several years and considered him a friend.

She smiled as she recalled that time in her life. "The complete answer was 'Yes, he's at the Omni Hotel in Atlanta.'"

"Was there a reason for him to be in Atlanta at that time?"

Sidney shook her head. "No, absolutely none in fact. I was completely sure that I had just made up the whole thing out of my own imagination and decided that I didn't need to be drinking eggnog at holiday time. I rolled over and went to sleep. Pretty much forgot about it on the spot."

Terrence knew what she was saying was true. Jensen was one of the most responsible men he was acquainted with. He wasn't the type that would just up and vanish for a couple of days, especially when he took care of his daughter as often as he did. He clearly remembered asking Jensen along on a "guys only" weekend several years ago after he'd broken up with Leslie. Jensen wouldn't come with them even though it wasn't his week to keep Kyra. He wanted to be close by in case he was needed. Not too many full-time fathers had the dedication Jensen did so he wouldn't just hop up and disappear for more than a few hours at most. But the twinkle in Sidney's eyes begged to be investigated further.

"But...?"

She burst into a big smile then. "But, the next night the TV show *Daily Access* came on. We were to be one of the featured stories that night but during the middle of our segment, they cut away to a live press conference featuring Mocha..."

He sat forward once more. "I remember that, but..."

"Jensen was standing behind him on the platform at the Omni Hotel."

He was somewhat impressed but wouldn't show it. He figured it best to keep the conversation going. "Ok, so how did you handle it?"

She gave a throaty chuckle and he decided that he liked her voice. "Not very well, I'm afraid. I freaked out and ran from the room."

"Understandably."

"Yes, Sidra and her friend Liz thought I was shaken by seeing a lawyer, who I thought was on my side, standing with my accuser. And I was but I was having more trouble processing the notion that the God who created the universe would take time to have a conversation with me... who hadn't acted like a saint since grade school."

"So you accepted Jesus right then and there, huh?" The story was plausible but he still had his doubts.

"Not exactly. First I worked myself into a migraine headache. I think it was a day or two later that I accepted Him into my life."

"That is a very interesting story, Sidney"

Her eyes were big when she signaled her agreement. "I know right. Who would have thought God actually wants to talk to us."

He knew he shouldn't have bothered but his curiosity was getting the better of him now. "Do you still dialogue with God?"

"Yes. Not every night or even every month, but we talk."

Terrence was silent. It all sounded good and he had no misgivings that she believed what she was saying but his life had been too hard. He had seen too much pain and despair, in his life and around the world and couldn't comprehend even wanting to speak to a God who allowed such atrocities to go on day after day.

"Sidney look, I'm happy for you. I really am but there's a lot I just don't get. I'm not sure I even want to know some things."

She sighed, "I understand. I truly do. I simply wanted you to know where I was coming from. So when I say things that may not seem to make any sense at the moment, give me a little lee-way, OK?"

Past experience had taught him well and he knew better than to agree to something so vague. "Things like what?"

"Like, what if I told you I know you didn't just randomly show up at the health expo or walk up to me tonight. You were sent to protect me."

He sat motionless, had even stopped breathing at some point. No one had ever picked up on his cover before. Not once. It was one of the things he prided himself on. If he needed to be a drug dealer or a diplomat or a charming ladies man, he became that person. He had a natural ability to blend into every possible demographic. So how did this one woman with no background in espionage pick up on him so easily? His senses went on high alert and he felt like he had just been busted in a sting.

Clearing his throat brought no relief from the things he was feeling so he grabbed his glass and took a long swallow. When he was sure he could speak in a normal tone he set the glass back on the table. "Why would you say something like that?"

"God told me."

"What else did He tell you?"

She gave a furtive grin. "Nothing else about you so you can relax."

He wiped his brow, only half jokingly. "Now you're starting to freak me out."

"Understandably."

When he recovered, he grilled her. "OK, seriously, what do you know?"

She offered a small shrug. "Not much honestly. Just that some strange happenings have been going on."

"Tell me."

"You first. Who are you?"

She had managed to raise both his eyebrows and that hadn't happened in a very long time. He had seriously underestimated the lovely lady across from him but he was a quick study and it wouldn't happen again. He realized then that he was going to have to keep not just an eye but two eyes on her at all times. *She would make a great agent.*

"Uh, wow. OK, My name really is Terrence and I work with Justice."

A small frown appeared on her face. "The Department of Justice or..."

They said it together, "Jensen's brother."

"Yeah, he asked me to keep an eye on you."

"Why?"

"You were about to tell me, remember? Strange happenings?"

She shook her head. "Smooth, very smooth."

He couldn't believe he was about to admit this but he did it anyway. "You almost penetrated my usually unflappable exterior. The first time ever, but if I hear that anywhere else, I'll deny it."

She laughed a heartfelt and cheerful laugh. "You don't have to worry, I'm pretty good at keeping secrets. That thing about my asking God about Jensen, you're the first one to hear it, ever."

"Good to know. Now, strange happenings?"

"Oh, right. Well someone has been hacking into my email accounts."

"How do you know?"

"At first, I had friends or co-workers who would say something like I sent you an email the other day but I would never get them. I knew something was up when I signed up for Facebook and I would get messages from my friends, mostly male, saying I can't add you as a friend. I made up an account, a fake guy friend and sent a request to myself. You know how you get an email every time someone sends a friend request?"

"I don't have an account, but yeah, I know."

Sidney stopped for a moment to look at him. "What do you mean you don't have a Facebook account?"

He leaned forward and whispered in a conspiratorial manner "let's just say the people I work for aren't all that excited about people like me constantly posting my whereabouts or what I'm thinking for the world to see."

"Oh, right."

"So, you were saying...?"

"Right, that email never came. Since then, I've had people on Facebook that I'm supposed to know say certain things that just don't feel right.

I've blocked a lot of them. The problem is I keep changing the passwords but whoever it is always gets back in. I know this because even though I won't have added any friends, my friend count can go up or down at a moments notice, even while I'm online."

He nodded. "Hmm, anything else?"

"Oh, plenty! Every now and then, my aunt needs to leave the house and insists I go with her. She moves excruciatingly slow on these trips where she's normally very mobile."

"Like she's giving someone time to get something done at the house."

"Exactly. Then there's the sticker that appeared in my windshield for an oil change I never got. The mileage written on the sticker had been pushed forward from what I actually needed."

"So, if you hadn't been paying attention, the car could have stopped in the middle of nowhere needing oil and you would thought the oil level was fine." *And been susceptible to any nut who drove up behind you.*

"Yes. Also, random men from the church will appear when I'm out at a restaurant or even getting my car worked on. They will speak to the mechanics but then make sure to let everyone see that they know me. And lets not forget the items in the house that keep disappearing."

He was blown away, first that she even recognized all of this was going on, but the level of detail she recalled was even more impressive. He was sure the men showing up at the service stations were there to make sure none of the mechanics tipped her off about the recently removed GPS located under her car. One well placed comment from a 'brother' or 'father' would be enough to stop a notification. This was worse than he thought.

"What type of items?"

"Jewelry I don't wear often, a few cosmetics and toiletries, programs from my computer."

He looked thoughtful. "What else."

"Well, every person labeled "pastor" on twitter ends up un-following me after a few weeks, I don't know what they may be hearing or getting but it's obvious someone is feeding them something about me."

"Something that is apparently believable." He sighed in frustration.

"Apparently. Also my mail seems to be unusually delayed... oh and I've also had people, from acquaintances to old friends call me and ask random questions or keep me on the phone when they really had nothing to say just to keep me talking... If I didn't know any better I would think they're being paid for it."

"Seriously?"

"Yeah but wait, there's more. Someone hacks into at least one of my email accounts on a daily basis now. And I don't get phone calls on my cell anymore. People have said they call my cell and get a message saying the phone has been disconnected or is not in service." She paused to look at him, deciding whether she should tell him what she was thinking. At this point, she had nothing to lose so she did. "Whatever this thing started out to be, it no longer is that. It's out of control, more than they realize."

He was almost afraid to ask the question but her last statement told him he needed her to confirm what he was thinking. "You know who it is don't you?"

"Yes."

He sat immobile for a several seconds. "And where is your God in all this?"

"Waiting."

"For?"

"His child to come to his senses. Like it or not, God loves him as much as He loves me"

The flash of anger that appeared in his eyes was instant. "See, that right there is why I won't bother with organized religion. Your God throws you to the wolves, wolves dressed in sheep's clothing and clerical collars and leaves you there to fend for yourself?"

He sent you. Sidney was about to say it out loud but the look on his face made her think now probably wasn't the best time. Instead she said, "Look, there are some things going on that you don't completely understand." She saw he was about to blow up again and steered the conversation into safer territory. "We can talk about it later but you should know I'm leaving Hearts Desire. A few weeks ago was my last Sunday there."

"Finally had enough huh?"

"He's recruiting."

"Recruiting who?"

"People ...or guys from my past. I ran into a guy at church a while back I used to be very close to. Apparently he's just started coming to Hearts Desire, had been for several weeks. He didn't say it, he didn't have to but I know he didn't just end up at that church by chance." She paused for a moment to let that sink in. "If he can't..."

Terrence was still seething. "He who, the wolf or the recruit?"

She sighed. "The wolf. If he can't get close to me, he'll get close to those who are or were close to me. I think this whole thing started off as a case of curiosity, mixed with a tinge of jealously perhaps. Others were invited in and now it's blown up into something he can't handle. I'm not even sure he knows how big it's become." *Or what kinds of demons are running it.*

He still couldn't figure why she was so calm about all of this but staring at her all night wouldn't give him the answer he wanted. Terrence snatched his wallet out of his back pocket and paid the bill before grabbing Sidney by the hand. "Come on. We need to go take care of some things at your house."

He had reached for her hand more out of his need to keep her close by and protect her than anything else. He was unaware of the looks and whispered comments as they strode by. Being one half of a beautiful couple was the last thing on his mind.

They parked her car at Terrence's place and she rode with him to her house. It was late and she didn't expect her elderly aunt to be awake at this time of night. It was no surprise that the only light burning was the front porch light.

Terrence stopped at the corner where she informed him he only had to make a right turn and stop in the middle of the block to find her house. He put the car in park and turned off the headlights. They watched as a dark sedan slowed down in front of Sidney's house, ever so slightly. Most people wouldn't have noticed it, but he did. He couldn't see the driver's face well but asked Sidney to slide down in her seat until the car passed them.

She was baffled. "What are we doing?"

"Waiting to make sure this is who I think it is. The car will make at least one more pass in front of your house if this is one of your wolves."

Sidney peered over what she could see of the dashboard and watched the car disappear into the shadows. "What happens if it is a wolf?"

"We let him know there's a new sheriff in town, one who likes to hunt wolves."

Just as he suspected, the car turned around and slowly made it's way back up the street. Terrence turned on his headlights as it passed them for the second time. It slowed momentarily but kept inching along. When he moved behind the car and followed for several yards the car nearly slowed to a crawl. When the car shifted ahead slightly, Terrence pulled up a little to back into Sidney's driveway. He thought the car might stop just ahead of her house but it kept going. He knew it would be back and he would be ready when it did. The micro camera sown into the baseball cap on his back seat would work nicely for what he had in mind. He put the hat on while he instructed Sidney to get her house keys out. Making his way around to open the door for his new charge, he waited patiently for the vehicle to return. Sidney's door was open but he stood looking down at her until he heard the faint hum of the car's engine.

Reaching for her hand, he waited as she placed it in his then pulled her up gently. He had her hand in his left one and was just closing her car door with the other when the mystery car pulled into full view. The car stopped directly in front of them. When Terrence looked into the tinted windows he saw the shape of a lone figure but nothing else. He pulled Sidney closer waiting for the car to move forward but it never did. He began to worry about her safety then. Either the person in the car was facing the end of his delusion or he was about to make a desperate attempt to reclaim it.

Terrence guided her to the end of the walkway and spoke quickly. "Get inside now, please. Hurry."

He turned back toward the car but reached for his weapon. He moved quickly towards the car but it sped off, tires screeching in protest. He ran after it, ensuring that the little camera above his head captured the whole tag number.

Sidney opened the door quickly when he knocked.

He was still breathing hard from chasing the car down the street and still angry. "I need to check your house for hidden cameras."

She nodded. There was nothing to say really. She'd had the feeling she was being watched and he just confirmed it. She put on a pot of coffee as she watched him check every corner of the house. He started to open the bedroom door on the lower level but Sidney caught him just in time.

"That's my aunt's room. I don't think you need to check in there."

The look he gave her said everything his mouth didn't. *Wolves are not to be trusted*. "I'll check it when she leaves."

The first virtue in a soldier is endurance of fatigue; courage is only the second virtue ~ Napoleon Bonaparte

CHAPTER 9

You're delusional, You're delusional. Boy you're losing your mind. It's confusing yo, You're confused you know. Why you wasting your time? Got you all fired up with your Napoleon complex. Seein' right through you, like you're bathing in Windex Oh, Oh, Oh. Boy why you so obsessed with me?

Mariah Carey's melodic voice sang out the words early Monday morning as if Sidney herself had penned them. Canaan stormed out of his home office and down the hall to his youngest son's bedroom. "Turn that trash off in this house! How many times do I have to tell you that we will play the Lord's music and only the Lord's music in this house!"

"Sorry Dad. This station plays gospel on Sunday mornings and I forgot it switched back during the week."

Realizing that his over-reaction to the lyrics was showing how out of control he really was he tried to reel the situation back in. "Oh... Well turn it down. We've got neighbors to think of."

As he sat down behind his desk the beleaguered pastor knew he had to do something. Seeing Sidney with that other man had stirred something in him, something he didn't know he was capable of exhibiting. The rage he felt the other night scared even him. All he could think was that he was turning into his father. He had often heard his mother referred to as a whore by that same man and he could never comprehend how a man who claimed to love a woman could call her out of her name. He understood now though. *How dare she take up with another man after all I would have sacrificed for her.*

After only meditating for a few moments, he knew what he had to do. It was clear that she shouldn't be away from him ever again for any length of time. He couldn't risk it. He was sure that the frenzy he had worked himself into only existed because she was inaccessible. He could get over this all-consuming need if she were closer. All he needed to do was get her out of his system and he knew only one way to do that. He had to bring her here with him.

He would build a room, a bunker of sorts in his basement and she could stay there. He had heard of other men taking women and keeping them in tiny little spaces with just a mattress on the floor. He would be better than that. He would fix

166

up the room like a hotel suite. She would be very comfortable. She probably wouldn't even want to leave after she arrived. He reached for his phone to call the deacon who could make it happen.

***

"Justice, I think he's completely lost it man. The car just stood there for almost a minute. It was like he couldn't come to grips with the fact that she was standing there with someone else."

"So you think it was Styles and not one of the subordinates?"

"Yeah, It was late and you only watch over something like that if you're vested and brother, whether he realizes it or not, he's vested."

"It was a dead tag. The former owner passed away only three weeks ago. It should've still been sitting on somebody's desk. How's Sidney holding up?"

Terrence shook his head. "Not well, man. I mean she keeps babbling something about warfare and I know she's getting antsy. I'm trying not to smother her but I just feel like this dude's on the edge. I won't let her out of my sight for more than a few hours."

"That's good because I think it's going to be a while before they bring him in. The more they dig, the more they find out but nothing they can use to get any serious prison time with. As it stands now, he'd only get a slap on the wrist for stalking but based on his connections, they're sure he's into something else. They're waiting for him to trip up big time and then pull the whole group in."

"There were six cameras in there man. It was like he needed to catch her from every possible angle. What about the idiot who gave him the surveillance equipment in the first place?"

"He's actually the reason we know so much to begin with. He came clean when Styles kept the equipment he was only supposed to need for a week. The guy kept going back asking for it and Styles kept handing him excuse after excuse."

Terrence snorted. "And that fool still works with us?"

Justice smiled through the phone at his friend. "You know how it works around here man, CYA! By the way, you're on assignment as far as I'm concerned. I'll handle it here if anyone starts asking questions."

He couldn't help laughing at his friend. "Yes sir!"

***

"Terrence this is ridiculous." He had just come out of Meena's bedroom searching for more cameras. "Nothing is going to happen to me."

"You're right. I'm going to make sure it doesn't."

Sidney sighed out of frustration. "You don't have to watch me like I'm five years old."

He gave a playful smile. "But I like watching you." When she glared at him he took a few steps closer. "Besides, I thought you liked spending time with me."

"You know I like spending time with you but this is..."

He pulled her by the hand until she was standing in front of him. "This is what's necessary to keep you safe. It should be over soon but I need you to work with me until then. Can you do that?"

"I guess so." The mumbled words were barely discernable but he responded with a "thank you" anyway. He really did hope that this would be over soon because quite honestly, he didn't know if he could take it much longer. While there was no way he could condone Style's stalking of her, he did see that there was something about her; something that made him feel connected to her in some way and something he wanted to explore further but couldn't because of the nature of this present relationship. He was already distracted because of her and that wasn't good. He almost sent up a silent prayer but suddenly thought better of it.

He released her hand, realizing he'd held it longer than needed. "Listen, how about you drop me at home on your way to the convention center and we can do dinner when you finish."

"You don't have to do this you know."

"Mm yeah, I know but I want to."

As they walked out into the bright afternoon sun, Terrence did his customary glance around the neighborhood to check out the surroundings. Had they stepped out the door a second sooner, he would have seen the car parked at the end of the street as it backed out of sight.

Officer Dirk Winston put the car in reverse just in a nick of time. There was something about the man that Sidney had been hanging out with. He couldn't put his finger on it but he knew the man was dangerous. He also knew it would be in everyone's best interest to get her away from him. When Pastor Styles called that morning and asked if he would be able to handle a small business transaction he jumped at the chance. "All you have to do is take her," he'd said. "I'll take care of the rest." Winston had an idea of what 'the rest' consisted of but if the good pastor thought he was going to be the only one to partake of the fruit from that garden, he was sadly mistaken. Winston reasoned that he wasn't going to do anything the pastor wasn't going to do and the man had called him his son in the ministry. *Like father, like son.*

Thirty minutes later he watched as Sidney dropped the man off at a luxury apartment building. Based on her schedule the last week and a half, he guessed she was headed back to the convention center and when she turned onto New York Avenue, he knew he was right. If a move was going to be made, it needed to be soon. He followed her into the parking garage and waited for her to park but he made the mistake of pulling into an empty space when he saw that she had paused to let a car pull out in front of her. He had his ski mask on in record time but he did not count on Sidney seeing him. When she saw that the other vehicle was moving slowly she laid on her horn. The driver of the minivan looked annoyed until she saw the masked man approach from behind and she peeled away. Sidney was right behind her. They made it to the next level but another car was backing out ahead of them and the man cut across the parking lot and broke Sidney's rear window with a toolbar just as she was about to pull away. The can of pepper spray lying in her driver's side door is the only thing that allowed her to escape, that and the grace of God.

Sidney tried to call Terrence from the police station but couldn't get through from her phone. That had been happening a lot lately. Seems that no one could call in or out from the number. She ended up sending him a text message. He barreled through the doors of the precinct about 15 minutes later to scoop her up in a big bear hug. He never mentioned to the local officers who he was or where he worked, just thanked them for filing the report and ushered her to his car.

He pulled into a hotel later that evening and waited for the valet. When he got out and escorted Sidney into the lobby she looked at him like he had lost his mind.

"What are we doing here?"

"We're spending the night. Think of it as a mini-vacation."

"I don't want to spend the night here!"

Terrence knew she was on edge and tired. He knew that's why her voice had just risen several octaves above its' normal tone. But her little outburst guaranteed that they were now the main attraction in the lavish lobby. He took a deep breath and tried to think of the best way to calm her down and at the same time ensure those who had witnessed the eruption that he wasn't holding Sidney against her will. He needed to make it upstairs without causing a scene but judging by the look on her face, it wasn't going to be easy. He walked toward her slowly with his palms up and he spoke low enough so that only she could hear.

"Sidney, please be reasonable. They are watching your house and expecting you to come back tonight. We need to figure out exactly what's going on and get prepared. We can go back tomorrow when we know it's safe."

She was on the verge of tears. He was standing only inches away from her now and when he saw she was about to break, he opened his arms and she walked right into them. The embrace did wonders for the audience in the lobby who went back to their routine when they saw that she was consolable. Terrence booked a suite for the night and rushed her upstairs after purchasing pajamas and toiletries in the gift shop. Room service and a rented movie finished the evening and she retired quietly. He watched her go and wondered if she were alright. She hadn't said much since they checked in but he figured she was probably just dazed from the afternoon's events.

He called her house to let Meena know she wouldn't be home until morning. He knew the older woman thought they were dating so he made it sound like something he had been planning for a while. He was more than surprised to hear Meena say that she had almost been the victim of a hit and run accident this evening. "But thank God the car swerved at the last second then took off down the road." She neglected to mention it happened right after she had received a visit from an angry young cop turned minister with swollen eyes. Dirk had shown up after the botched attempt with Sidney and threatened to arrest her and throw her in prison if she didn't contact him immediately after she heard from Sidney. She figured she didn't need to bother Sidney's young man with that, just warn him to be cautious on the road.

Terrence hung up the phone and massaged his neck for a few moments. If they had attempted to take Sidney and wipe out Meena in the same day that only added up to trouble. When he was sure Sidney was settled, he called Justice so the security tapes from the garage could be retrieved and reviewed.

"I don't like it."

Justice agreed with his friend. "Me either. They're ramping up."

"Wait a second..."

"What is it?"

Terrence slapped himself for overlooking the obvious. Of course they had inside help. Their surveillance of Sidney could only be as extensive as it was because Meena was helping them. "If they're trying to get rid of Meena maybe we can do some snooping of our own and use that to our advantage."

"That's a good idea but I've also been thinking, if they're trying to take Sidney, they must have a place in mind to hold her, otherwise why go for the grab. I'll get someone over there to bug Sidney's house tonight, then give me some time to do my own snooping. We might be able to close this up sooner than I thought."

"Cool."

Before the sun was up the next morning, Terrence received a text from Justice. 'Same tag from the other night but different car.'

Ten days later they were back at her house and she was going stir crazy. She could not make a move without Terrence being right by her side and she was sick of it and him. He tried to explain it to her but she didn't really care. All she wanted was her life back. She grumbled and complained and scowled at the new houseguest who had taken over her sofa. But try as she might, he would not be moved. He just smiled when she scowled and took up his nightly post on the sofa. He had seen it all before.

Later that evening, Terrence got a 'heads up' text from the agent sitting in a car down the street from Sidney's house. Damaris stood on the porch knocking loudly and waiting impatiently. When Sidney finally opened the door, Damaris tried to step in but Sidney wouldn't let her.

"Hey Sid! What's up?" The emotions behind the words were overly cheerful and forced. Both women knew it.

"Hey, nothing but I wish you would have called first because now is not a good time."

"Oh, no problem I just wanted to check on you because, well I didn't want to mention this but there's a rumor going around church that you have recently shacked up with some man and are living in sin." She said all this while doing her best to get an eye full of what she could see in the house.

Sidney pressed her lips into a straight line. "Well, you know how some church people are, ready and willing to spread the good news and gossip. The truth is I have a friend staying with me, that's all. No more, no less. Oh and I must have forgot to mention that I'm no longer attending Hearts Desire. "

"Oh?" Damaris eyes were wide and she looked hungry for any bit of information she would be able to pass on. "What church are you attending now?"

"I haven't decided yet." It was a lie and Sidney asked for forgiveness as soon as the words crossed her lips. She had settled on Tabernacle of

Faith, Sidra's old church and the church where her mentor, Pastor Cyrus attended. She just hoped and prayed Pastor Johnson had more discernment than other Christians she'd come across recently.

Still miffed that she wouldn't be let inside, Damaris shrugged her shoulders. "OK, I'm just saying, the bible says to abstain from the appearance of evil and you don't look like you're abstaining from anything."

"Yeah well, that can't be helped right now. Thanks for stopping by." Sidney shut the door quickly and almost ran upstairs to her room.

Terrence felt bad for her and told Justice as much when he picked up his ringing cell phone.

"I wouldn't waste my time feeling bad about it if I were you." Justice was short and to the point as usual. "Her friend is hardly worried about impropriety when she and the pastor's son have been going at it like rabbits. She's also the main point of contact between Sidney and Styles, or at least she was until Sid cut her back but that's not why I called."

Terrence straightened up at that last remark. "What'd you find?"

Justice sighed before recounting his findings. "Styles is preparing what looks to be a fallout shelter in his basement- a sound proof room with a secret entrance that will be completely hidden from view."

Terrence could not believe what he was hearing. "You're serious?"

Justice sighed again. "I'm afraid so. Satellite images don't lie. It looks like he's setting up for a long-term guest and by the looks of things the room, or I should call it a suite really, is about ready."

Terrence was too stunned to be angry but that only lasted for a moment. "God help us. So he was planning to go preach on Sunday mornings then return home to ..." He didn't even want to finish the sentence, much less the thought. "What is the world coming to?"

"Indeed, and while we can't arrest him for building a shelter we can and will charge him with a planned kidnapping. We've got people already on it. All we need is something written or even verbal from the wiretap confirming his plans to kidnap and hold Sidney and we can put that idiot away for the length of time he deserves. Hell, I'd even settle for the guy who tried to snatch her. We can build a case around that."

Terrence didn't realize that the volume on his cell phone was turned all the way up or that Sidney was standing in the doorway listening to every word. When he turned and saw her she walked away and he ended the call quickly.

"Uh, Just man, I got to go. I'll give you a call back later."

He found her rocking back and forth in front of the fireplace. He sat down next to her and stayed quiet for several minutes. When she didn't say anything, he decided to. "How much did you hear?"

"Enough."

"I'm really sorry about that. I should have been more careful."

"It doesn't matter, it's fine."

He turned to watch her as she looked at the fire. "Someone you considered a good friend is selling you out to a crazy man who's planning to kidnap you and hold you hostage and God only knows what else. There is no one close to you that you can trust. Sidney it's not fine."

She never answered him. She simply stood up and walked upstairs to her room. Once upstairs she tried to sleep but sleep wouldn't come. Anger came though and so did depression and she opened the door and let them in. It was a reunion of sorts. The same spirits that had plagued her several years earlier were back but they seemed stronger this time. She didn't fight them, just laid there and let them come in.

*   *   *

Sidney couldn't take it anymore. She waited for almost 30 minutes after the lights went out and made sure it was quiet before she made her move. She had oiled the hinges on her bedroom door in anticipation of just such an event. She grabbed her keys out of her purse and slowly walked toward the front door. Her right hand had just turned the locks in the right direction to leave out and her hand was slowly turning the doorknob to the right when she felt his presence He was in the room with her.

By the time he reached the doorknob she had already removed her hand and turned to face him. He was barely holding his anger in check and she could feel the tension radiating from him. They stood about 3 inches apart. He didn't speak for several seconds, not until he got control of his temper.

"Where are you going?"

"Out."

He stepped forward to lock the door again. "Nice try."

Sidney was not deterred. She purposely raised her voice and said "I am not staying in this house one more minute."

"Keep your voice down! You're going to wake your aunt."

"You're the one standing here arguing, I'm on my way out."

She reached for the doorknob even as she felt her hand being engulfed by his larger one a moment later. "I can't let you do that."

Sidney had reached her end. She yelled out her next words like she was in a stadium. "You don't have to let me do anything! I'm a grown woman and I can take care of myself!"

He didn't mean to curse in her house but he was exasperated with this woman who seemed to care nothing for her life. He scooped her up as if she were a child and walked over to the sofa. Sidney kicked and struggled all the way across the room.

"Put me down!"

"Fine." He plopped down on the sofa with Sidney in a vice grip on his lap. "You're down."

Sidney was so mad she was almost in tears. "This is not funny Terrence."

"No it's not. In fact, I would love to hear why you're so willing to offer up your life to these idiots." When she didn't say anything he turned her on his lap until they were face to face. "Sidney, these people are certifiably crazy. They are trying to snatch you and if that doesn't work they won't have any problem killing you. This is not something you should be taking lightly."

After several moments she was still silent and her eyes were closed but he knew she was listening because a tear escaped out of the corner of her eye. She wiped it away quickly and slowly opened both eyes.

What he saw looking back was emptiness. A pair of empty eyes set in a lovely face. It startled him because he had only seen that look before in two places on the planet. He had seen it once in Serbia and again in the women and children of Darfur when he was sent on a brief mission there a few years ago. Vacant eyes were a tell tale sign of a disconsolate soul. The thing that worried him though was that for all the intensity he had seen coming from her earlier, he saw nothing now. There was no fight left. The only thing he saw looking back at him was complete defeat. This from a girl Justice had called "fiery" was not right. There was obviously something deeper going on here. Something he had missed and he thought, it appeared to have been going on for some time for her to look like this. The next words out her mouth confirmed his observations.

"I don't care anymore." She spoke quietly, empty eyes begging him to understand. "They're not crazy and I don't want to live like this another minute."

He gently grabbed both sides of her face. "What are you saying?"

"I'm saying I'm done trying. There's no end to it – ever. I should just take care of the situation once and for all and I'll be free."

"Sidney, I'm trying to understand here but you need to help me out. What are you trying to tell me?"

She laid her head on his chest but she never answered him. How could she explain to a man who questioned the very existence of God the concept of spiritual warfare? How could she tell him that she would be hunted for the rest of her days by an unseen enemy; who, judging by the last few months, would always have the upper hand over her and apparently anyone who got too close to her. Where would she be able to find the words to say that the spirit of suicide that had beguiled her into attempting to take her life a few years earlier was knocking at the door again and this time she was ready to swing open the door and invite it in to finish the job. She never opened her mouth. She couldn't. She just cried it all out while she sat on the lap of the bewildered federal agent.

There's a time to pray but there's a time to speak. You don't pray about your mountains, you speak to your mountains. You command them to go... Your mountain responds to your voice. ~ Joel Osteen

CHAPTER 10

Jensen sat straight up in bed...He looked over at his wife who looked so peaceful in her sleep. He decided not to wake her but his spirit was in turmoil. He eased out of bed and quickly made his way downstairs where there were no sleeping family members to awaken. Something was wrong with someone he cared about and he felt like he needed to help in some way. He knelt down in front of the sofa and began to call on God. *God please show me what I need to know to help.* Immediately, he saw a vision of Sidney being attacked by two large hideous beasts. The sword she'd been holding had been dropped long ago and she was curled up in a fetal position on the floor while the two beasts stomped, kicked, poked and pulled at her. He saw that she had no help around her and that she was slowly but surely giving up.

He started praying right away but he felt like he needed to do more. He quietly ran back upstairs and got dressed. For the five minutes it took for him to put his clothes on he debated whether to wake Sidra or not. Knowing his wife the way he did, he knew she would have jumped up straight away to join him. Now, though, they had three children to think of and they couldn't just pick up and take off like they did when it was just the two of them. He was about to leave a note on the pillow when wisdom spoke and said to wake her.

He shook her gently at first but when she didn't stir he used a little more force. She finally opened her eyes and seeing the look on her husbands face, sat straight up. "What's wrong?"

"Sidney's in trouble and I need to get over there."

"What? Wait? How do you know?" She had opened her eyes but she wasn't fully awake yet.

"God just showed me. Now baby listen, I need you to trust me, all right? We can take the time to pack up all the kids and risk losing this fight or I can go alone with your blessing and speak life into the situation. The choice is yours."

The first thing that popped into Sidra's mind was a picture of Sidney kissing Jensen. She let it linger only a second before she shook her head to clear the thought. "Go. I'll be here praying for you."

The kiss lasted several seconds. "I love you so much right now."

Sidra smiled and kissed him once more. "You better, now go get my sister." Jensen grabbed his keys and raced out the front door toward his SUV. Not one minute had passed by before Sidra heard the sly voice in her head. *What if she kisses him again? What if he can't resist this time?* Sidra was irate at the gall of the enemy. She recognized the voice for what it was and practically hollered out "Shut up devil!!" She sat straight up in the bed, closed her eyes and began to pray for her sister and then her husband. When she opened her eyes again, she saw Kyra standing in the doorway with eyes as big as saucers and looking absolutely petrified.

Sidra's heart fell when she realized she must have woken her daughter with her outburst. She stretched her arm out and smiled. "I'm sorry I woke you baby. Come help me pray for your Auntie. God told your Daddy to go check on her." The little girl scrambled up into the large bed in a flash. Before they got started Sidra pulled her big girl closer and noticed she was shivering slightly. She had Kyra come closer so they could snuggle under the covers together. "Are you still cold?"

Kyra shook her head and spoke in a whisper. "I wasn't cold before. I just thought it was happening again. But I understand now. Come on let's pray for Auntie Sidney."

Being the experienced attorney she was, Sidra West was rarely caught off guard, either in her professional life or her personal life; but her nine year old had just managed to do it without any effort at all. The little girl was right of course. They needed to pray for Sidney but Sidra made a mental note to check with Kyra in the morning about the 'I thought it was happening again' part of her last statement. She grabbed the small pair of hands and started. "Father God..."

It was 3:00 a.m. when Jensen pulled onto the highway. Because he had no traffic to contend with on the way over to Sidney's place he knew it would be a fairly short ride. He called her cell phone when he pulled up in front of the house but heard a message that the number was no longer in service. He didn't want to but he had no other choice than to reach for the doorbell. He remembered Sidney was a sound sleeper but also remembered Ms. Meena was staying there. He didn't want to wake the elderly woman but he knew he needed to get in there. He had just touched the doorbell again when the door swung open.

"Terrence?"

Jensen had only a short time to process what was going on before strong arms pulled him inside. "She won't wake up!"

"What?"

"She won't wake up!"

Jensen looked toward the sofa and saw that his sister-in-law was motionless. He walked toward her trying to discern if he were dealing with a physical malady or a spiritual problem. He looked over at Terrence and said with some urgency. "Go upstairs and check her medicine cabinet. Make sure there are no empty prescription bottles lying around. He didn't know what Terrence knew about Sidney's past or what he was doing here but he knew if Terrence was here, his brother was involved. And if Justice was involved that meant Sidney was in trouble. He knelt down by the sofa and grabbed her hand.

"Sidney? Sidney, honey can you hear me?" She stirred just enough to let Jensen know she was alive but he still didn't know whether or not she was in a demonic battle or a drug induced haze. Terrence had just raced back down the steps to report that the only thing she had was over-the-counter medication. That wasn't extremely helpful because Jensen knew that people over-dosed on OTC's all the time. Since he didn't know what to do, there was only one thing to do. He stepped up to the plate with a big stick in his hands.

"I plead the blood of Jesus over this house and everything in it. In the name and by the authority of the Lord Jesus Christ, the son of the living God, I command every evil spirit and force of darkness to loose this child of God right now!" Jensen took a step back when Sidney sat straight up gulping for air.

When she opened her eyes they were brimming with tears and filled with pure defeat. "They're winning" was all she said.

Jensen had been given the answer he was looking for. This was war and if the devil wanted to pick a fight, then he was ready to oblige him. He snatched Sidney up off the sofa so fast it took what little breath she had away. "No they are not!"

He yelled so loud that Meena had come awake and cracked open her bedroom door to see what was going on. Jensen continued to hold Sidney up and pray. "Devil you have no authority in this house or over this vessel!"

Sidney was crying outright now. "Jensen just let them take me. It will be better this way."

"Sidney Rochelle Lyons!" Upon hearing her full name, she sobered up and looked at the man she had come to love like a brother. "I'm tired of fighting with no help."

That was the first sign to him that the Sidney he knew was back. "Sweetie, you don't have to fight alone any more. I came here to help you fight."

Sidney looked up and Terrence who was standing by Jensen saw just a glimmer of what he hadn't seen all night. He saw hope. Terrence felt like he should pray or something but given their earlier conversations, he knew he was out of his league. He did manage a silent *God help her* but stepped back out of the way to watch Jensen do his thing.

Jensen and Sidney hit their knees and started to pray. Terrence watched as Jensen put one hand on Sidney's head. He started to pray for

Sidney and Sidney started to pray in a language he didn't understand. Not that he was an expert on every language spoken on the planet but he knew enough of the major ones to know that she wasn't saying anything he had ever heard before. Five minutes into the prayer the lights began to flicker and he heard Jensen say something about taking authority over the darkness. The lights came back on.

That was the point where Terrence knew he had stepped into some deep, next level stuff. The praying went on for about twenty minutes more when they stopped and he heard Sidney say "devil you have already been defeated and you will not keep me from my destiny. In the authority and in the name of the Lord Jesus Christ, I command you to go and release your hold on my life! You have no place here." A peaceful calm settled over the house and Terrence physically felt something, a presence or something in the room but he didn't dare move.

When Sidney stood up she began singing in perfect Japanese. It was a song he had heard the villagers sing many a day on the side of the large mountain. He couldn't believe what he was hearing. Eventually she stopped singing, opened her eyes and said "kishi kaisei, shinobi" Literally: 'Wake from death and return to life, shinobi.' He couldn't count the number of times he'd heard the old sensei in the village say that to him. He knew though, it had a different meaning now. The word 'shinobi' had pretty much assured him that God was speaking directly to him through Sidney. He was an experienced agent. He had seen some things, even supernatural things that he just didn't understand but this message was loud and clear.

Jensen nodded and said "amen" after Sidney finished speaking. When Terrence looked at him, Jensen just shrugged his shoulders. "I have no idea what she said but it sounded serious." Terrence thought about laughing but he was afraid to move. He looked to Sidney who nodded at him also. "I have no idea what I said either but judging by the look on your face, you do. And going by what I just felt, God was serious when He said it so I'm thinking there's a decision to be made here."

There was no desperation in her eyes now only tranquility and peace. She looked as if she had just won the heavy weight title. Terrence looked around the nicely decorated house, took a deep breath in and slipped out of the chair and onto his knees while looking at his two companions. "I want what you have."

Smiling faces looked down on him. "We can take care of that right now." Jensen and Sidney joined him on their knees while Jensen led him in prayer.

"It's as easy as repenting for your sins and inviting Jesus into your heart. You ready?"

"Yeah. So...this is a one time deal right? One of my foster mothers used to get saved every Sunday."

Sidney tried to hide a smile.

Jensen grabbed his friend's shoulder and looked straight into his eyes. "Jesus said no one would be able to pluck us out of His hand, and while learning to live how God wants us to is a process, once you truly accept Him into your life as Savior and Lord, you're sealed for all eternity."

Terrence nodded. "O.K. Let's do this."

Jensen began. "Just repeat after me. God I know that I am a sinner. I repent and ask for your forgiveness."

Terrence closed his eyes, took a deep breath and repeated the words.

"I believe that Jesus Christ is the Son of God,"

Jensen waited to hear Terrence say the words before he continued. "I believe that Jesus Christ came to earth and was crucified to pay for my sins and the sins of all mankind."

He repeated, "I believe that Jesus Christ came to earth and was crucified to pay for my sins and the sins of all mankind."

Sidney reached for his hand as Jensen continued to lead him in the prayer.

"I believe that Jesus Christ was raised from the dead and now has all power."

Terrence went on. "I believe that Jesus Christ was raised from the dead and now has all power."

Jensen smiled at his friend. "This is the last part. I accept Jesus as my Savior and the Lord of my Life."

Terrence took a gulp of air then said, "I accept Jesus as my Savior and the Lord of my Life."

Sidney gave him a quick hug before she added. "Father we thank You for sending the Holy Spirit to lead and guide him. Please allow him to grow in wisdom and in faith, in Jesus name I ask amen."

When they stood to their feet, Jensen grabbed him into a bear hug. "Welcome to the family man."

Tears misted his eyes. Terrence finally had the family he had longed for. "Thanks man."

Jensen scooped Sidney up next. "Sis, you gonna take care of the whole Romans Road thing? I need to get out of here and get back to my other family."

She hugged him back hard. "I got it. Go home."

She grabbed his coat off the sofa and walked him to the door. "Jensen. Thank you."

"That's what family is for. Night, sis."

"Good night."

When she turned around, Terrence was staring at her, expectantly. "What's the Roman's Road?"

"Several passages of scripture that explain who Jesus is, what He did for us and how we should accept Him. Most people hear that before they get saved but considering the circumstances, we'll just have to go out of order tonight."

"I'm different."

Sidney laughed and nodded her agreement. "Yes you are. Hold tight. I'll go get my bible and we can go over it."

"Good, I want to hear everything, including how you managed to sing and speak perfect Japanese tonight."

"Hmm. I think I may need to put on a pot of coffee then."

"Yeah, you might need two because I've got a ton of questions."

Sidney smiled. "OK, I'll answer what I can and we'll find someone for you to talk to about the rest."

***

Jensen returned home to find Kyra and Sidra asleep in the bed. He kissed Sidra to let her know he was back but she didn't stir so he slid under the covers and closed his eyes.

The sunshine seemed to invade the room a few minutes later. Sidra rose quietly and got the twins fed and changed before she woke Jensen. She walked around to his side of the bed so she wouldn't disturb Kyra and kissed him until his eyes opened.

"Good Morning"

"Good Morning to you. How did it go last night?"

Jensen smiled remembering how he left Terrence and Sidney last night. "Superb"

She smiled back. "Good. Are you going into work this morning?"

He closed his eyes again. "I'm really thinking about calling in. There's nothing pressing going on at the moment."

"I think you should call in, then take the babies over to my mom's. Kyra's going to school late today."

"Why what's wrong?" He looked down at the small sleeping form curled up next to him.

"Nothing we can't straighten out over breakfast. But she was up late so you have time to get cleaned up and drop the twins off. I'll shower and start breakfast while you're gone. And then we can spend the rest of the day together.'

"Sounds like a plan to me."

As soon as the twins were strapped into their car seats, Jensen had his cell phone out of his pocket. Justice picked up on the second ring.

"Hey bro you at work?"

"No, we're an hour behind you guys remember? I've still got some time. What's up?"

Jensen pulled his shades on while he slid behind the wheel. "I was just about to ask you the same thing."

"What do you mean?"

"I ran into Terrence at Sidney's last night."

"Oh. That."

"Yeah, that."

"I can't say a lot. I mean I can't go into details right now but I will say that you need to pray."

"You're telling me to pray?" As far as Jensen knew, his brother was an agnostic. If Justice was saying he needed to pray, things were worse than he thought. "Brother, you just said a mouthful."

Jensen took the twins over to Sidra's mom's house and arrived back home in time to find Sidra setting three places for breakfast. He hugged her from behind when he reached the table.

"Pancakes and waffles. This must be serious."

Kyra turned the corner just as he finished speaking

Sidra smiled at their oldest child before turning to whisper in her husband's ear. "We're about to find out."

"Come on Ky, dig in. We need to get you to school by third period for the day to count."

As Kyra stuffed waffles in her mouth, Sidra started to talk. "Ky, last night, when you said 'I thought it was happening again.' What did you mean?"

"Well, when I heard you yelling last night it woke me up and it scared me because it sounded like mommy and Don. The last time it happened they were yelling a lot and the next day I was living with you and Daddy."

She stopped to swallow her mouthful of food before continuing. "I thought you were yelling at Daddy but then you explained it and I understood."

Jensen looked over at Sidra. "Who were you yelling at?"

Sidra answered Jensen but kept her eyes on Kyra. "One thing at a time sweetie, hmm?" She really didn't want to admit to the thoughts she had allowed to enter her mind last night, especially in front of Kyra.

"Ky did your mommy tell you why you were coming to live with your daddy and me?"

"No, but she didn't' have to. I knew it was my fault."

Jensen was still trying to figure out whom his wife could have been yelling at when his daughter's words finally registered.

"Whoa, what? Pumpkin, what was your fault?"

"The reason Mommy and Don were fighting all the time so she sent me here so they could stop."

Sidra was just as perplexed as Jensen. "How did you come to that conclusion Ky?"

"Because all they did was yell when they were together but every time I walked into the room, they stopped and got quiet. So it had to be my fault."

Jensen shook his head. "No baby, I think you got it wrong. They weren't yelling because of you and they didn't stop because you walked in the room. I'm pretty sure they stopped because they didn't want to worry you."

Kyra looked up at her father with big questioning eyes. "Then why were they fighting in the first place?"

Sidra reached across the table and covered the child's hand. "Grown-ups fight sometimes, that's all. That's just the way it is. And I know for a fact that your mommy loves you too much to send you away for something like that."

Tears fell freely down the young face as she listened to Sidra. "But she did! She sent me away!"

Jensen was up and at his daughter's side in a flash. He picked the girl up and placed her on his lap as he sat down in the chair she had just occupied. Her head fell against his chest as sobs racked her little body. "Baby, listen to me. Your mommy sent you here because she didn't want you to be around the fighting, that's all."

She was expectant when she looked up. "Are you sure?"

He nodded and smiled. "Positive."

"But..."

Sidra knew the little girl still had doubts, who wouldn't after thinking about something a certain way for a year. "Ky, how did you feel when you heard your mommy and Don fighting?"

"I didn't like it. It scared me."

Sidra nodded. "Your mommy knew that and didn't want you to feel bad, so she sent you here, where you wouldn't have to be around it."

"Oh." The light bulb had gone off and she looked up with new understanding.

Jensen squeezed her tight until she screamed out. "Daddy! I can't breathe!"

"Oh sorry, maybe this will help" He tickled her until she was laughing and crying uncle.

"OK, OK, I can breathe now."

"Good. And Ky, for the record there's nothing you can do that will make us send you away."

She smiled, feeling comforted. "Even if you start fighting and it's my fault?"

Sidra grabbed her hand and pulled her into a big bear hug. "Baby, if your daddy and I start fighting, it's going to be his fault but the family will never be broken up because of it."

"Never?"

"Nope, not ever."

Jensen arrived home after dropping Kyra off at school and found Sidra in the living room. He slid next to his wife on the sofa, pain clearly etched on his face. "I feel like such an idiot. She's been walking around here for almost a year, believing this was her fault."

"Hey, go easy on yourself." Sidra tried to rub his frown lines away. "We had no idea what she was thinking. We should have asked long before now but kids don't come with manuals. We did the best we could with what we had. Now we know better."

"Yeah, I guess you're right."

"Of course I am."

He suddenly remembered a comment brought up earlier that morning in the conversation. "Who were you yelling at in an empty house at 2:30 in the morning?"

Sidra sighed. "Oh, that"

"Is that the catch phrase for the morning?"

"Huh?"

"Nothing, something Justice said earlier."

"About Sidney?" When he nodded she sat straight up. "Tell me."

"Of course I will Love, right after you finish telling me what happened when I left this morning."

Tell the truth and shame the devil. ~ Big Mama

CHAPTER 11

Sidney and Terrence were on their third pot of coffee when sunlight came spilling into the house. She had been up all night answering all of the questions that Terrence asked. He studied everything she said with rapt attention and didn't hold back on his questions. She was happy to stay up with him but he had worn her out. He only recognized it when she yawned and sank back into the chaise.

"OK, second to the last question."

"Shoot."

"I'm not sure you know the answer but why does God allow all the evil in the world to continue?"

"The best answer I can give you is God gave man free will and established him as the ruler of this planet, He even put laws in place. Man dropped the ball and what you see around you is the result. If God came back and revoked free will, it would sort of defeat the purpose. Instead, He sent Jesus to offer an acceptable resolution and still keep our free will in tact. It is man that continually rejects God's option."

He nodded with understanding.

"I never thought about it like that. OK, I'm almost done but tell me this. Last night when I said, 'they're crazy' you said 'they're not crazy'. I know there was something else you didn't say last night. What was it?"

Sidney took a deep breath and sat up to look at her new friend. "It's one of the most controversial parts of Christianity and most people have taken to calling it spiritual warfare."

"Why controversial?"

"Because it involves the enemies of God and a lot of Christians don't believe that an actual devil exists."

"Something tells me you know better."

"I do."

"You want to share?"

"It's going to sound a little crazy, fantastical even."

"Sweetie, after the night I had, you could tell me anything and I would believe it."

"OK, you asked for it. You remember that movie, the one where the kid says 'I see dead people'?"

"Yeah, you see dead people?"

"I see demons, not often but I've seen enough to let me know that we are in an actual battle."

"But why you? I mean, how come everyone can't see them?"

"I honestly don't know. I think it may come with certain people's gift mix."

"Gift mix?"

Sidney stood up and shared at Terrence with alarm. "Oh no!"

He stood up with her and reached for the gun behind his back as he looked around the house. "What's wrong?"

"First, I need you to put your gun away. You'll figure out soon enough that there is no physical weapon that will work in spiritual warfare. Secondly, I can't believe I forgot to tell you about your spiritual gifts."

"I get gifts?"

"Yeah, you do. Everyone does after they accept Christ." She started for the staircase as she pointed for him to have a seat. "Sit tight and don't shoot anything while I'm gone. I'll be right back."

She came back down stairs with her laptop and two books. She set the laptop up next to him and pulled up a site on the web. "There are a few different tests out there but I like this one. It's a free test you take online. Just answer the questions and it will give you an idea of what your gift or gifts are."

He got started immediately but fell silent when the page was loading. "What are those?" he nodded to the two books sitting near her.

"These are books to help you get started on your walk with Christ. One is an introduction and explanation of the third member of the trinity, the Holy Spirit. The other is a breakdown of all the spiritual gifts. When you get your results back from the test, we can see what you're working with."

***

"It's a terrible thing to want something so badly that you're willing to play with the devil to get it.... In the end you'll find that you are the only one who gets played. You'd better hear what I'm saying and call upon the living God while you have time." Rev. Johnson looked out at his congregation with a solemn face. His spirit hadn't been settled for weeks. He knew trouble was brewing somewhere close but didn't know how close or how many people would be affected. The Lord had prompted him to fast and pray, and he had done just that for several days now but he was still ill at ease. He just hoped the mercy of God covered whatever and whoever was at risk. "Come on saints let's stand and pray."

Meena and Terrence had accompanied Sidney to her new church on this particular Sunday. Meena didn't say why she wanted to join them at church on Sunday but Sidney had a pretty good idea. After Terrence had gotten saved the other night, he revealed everything that the FBI knew about Sidney's case. He went down a list of several people that Sidney had suspected along with several others she didn't. Terrence explained that everyone involved would be held responsible for his or her actions. That included jail time for most of the people he had named, including Meena.

The thought of her aunt, spending any of her senior years locked up saddened Sidney but there was nothing she could do. Canaan Styles had pulled the wool over a lot of people's eyes, in the beginning at least. Terrence said the FBI had been watching for long enough to know that not many were working in the dark now. Many of them had a very good idea of what was going on, and that it was wrong. The fact that they didn't come forward to expose the crimes would not look good for any of them. The feds were ready to move in and end it. A lot of people would be charged with cyber-stalking or aiding and abetting a crime and would have to do the time for it.

She asked Terrence to help her pray for her aunt. He had said that if Meena came forward of her own accord before the feds exposed everything, she would stand a good chance at getting just probation with no jail time. "But if she doesn't, there really is no guarantee that a judge is going to take her age into consideration and let her off easy." Sidney had been praying for her aunt for several days now. She only had a short time left because Terrence said agents were gearing up to storm Canaan's church and home in the coming week.

Meena and Sidney waited until the sanctuary had cleared out before attempting to leave. Sidney looked over at her elderly aunt who had seemed to age 15 years in the last few months. Of course Sidney knew what was wrong but could only pray that her aunt came to the right conclusion before something terrible happened. "You ready Auntie?"

Meena tried to catch her breath but she just couldn't seem to breathe normally these past couple of weeks. That young fool had stressed her out. She knew she was carrying a burden she had no business holding on to. She decided to take the preacher's advice and put it in the hands of Jesus.

"Baby girl we need to talk and I think we should do it with the pastor present."

Sidney didn't think to hide her relief. She pulled the older woman into as big a hug as she could muster. "Yes, we do!" She sent up a silent *thank you* to the Lord above for moving on her aunt's heart.

***

The head of the precinct where Walker and Winston worked just happened to attend Tabernacle of Faith and was outside directing traffic for the huge church when Pastor Johnson called to see if he was still around. He was and met Sidney, Meena and Terrence in the pastor's office. Meena told them everything. Terrence was thankful because Meena's testimony about Winston having red swollen eyes on the day when Sidney was almost abducted meant that they could definitely charge Styles with kidnapping.

The police chief sat with his mouth open for most of the meeting. He couldn't believe what he was hearing. He had noticed Winston's red swollen eyes a couple of weeks ago but never imagined they were in that condition because he had attempted to commit a serious crime. He knew Officer Walker was a good man who had just gotten caught up in the wrong situation at the wrong time but heads would still have to roll. He sighed as he entered his patrol car. He was not looking forward to work tomorrow morning.

Officer Walker noticed the police station appeared to be unusually quiet when he stepped inside that morning. If he didn't know any better he'd swear that all eyes were on him. He reached his desk and pulled out his chair gingerly. Something was wrong. He didn't know what it was but he knew it was about to hit the fan. He didn't even jump when the Chief's voice bellowed across the precinct.

"Walker! Winston! Get in here!"

***

On Monday morning five black SUV's pulled into Canaan's driveway at 6:55am. One FBI agent pressed the doorbell and when Mrs. Styles opened the door, shoved a search warrant in her face and asked her to step outside. Of course she was flustered and shocked and all the things that go along with being surprised by the FBI early on a Monday morning but most of all, she was humiliated. They wouldn't even let her see Canaan. He was held in another room and then he and his sons were led out of the house in handcuffs for everyone to see. Someone had tipped a local news station so cameras were perched on the front lawn waiting to film every demeaning minute that would later be broadcast on the evening news.

Unfortunately, the same thing was happening across town on the grounds of the church. Agents in black jackets moved in and out of the church gathering boxes of paper, file cabinets and computers to load up and take away to be analyzed further. Of course Edna-Jean expressed shock and disdain for what the pastor had allegedly done. She was on the phone in a matter of moments calling for another prayer meeting.

***

Pastor Cyrus listened to the full account of happenings for the past several months and could only shake her head when the story was finished. She was quiet for several minutes as she surveyed the damage in her mind. Her thoughts went first to her embattled protégé. She reached out for Sidney's hand only imagining what she could have been going through and essentially alone. Sidney met her mentor's gaze with a steady one of her own. Sidney was afraid to speak because of the tears that were gathering but she was trying to let the older woman know that she was fine.

"All those lives damaged for... nothing." Pastor Cyrus looked at Sidney once more. "And you know the sad thing is, even had those young people done everything right, they still wouldn't have been ready for those demons your pastor ..." The look on Sidney's face caused her to stop mid sentence and she understood what the younger woman was thinking. "...Your former pastor introduced them to for at least another fifteen years. Now that thing has tried to settle in and take root. Lord have mercy! Opening the door to those types of spirits to people ignorant in spiritual ways is just asking for trouble. God only knows how many generations of those poor families will be influenced." She shook her head again. "Mm, mmm, mmph! I'm going to call them out in my prayer time and pray God has mercy on their souls."

Sidney agreed solemnly. "They are going to need it."

"Yes, see baby this is what I was trying to get you to understand about authority. Whatever authority Canaan Styles had to speak into the lives of others is now severely diminished, if not destroyed all together. It's our authority the enemy is after and he can't take it from us so he tricks us into giving it up."

***

Another season had ended and Sidney wasn't sure what to make of it or her life. She had been in and out of turmoil since accepting Christ as her Savior and she was ready for a break from the stress. She planned on taking one too, just as soon as she let her sister and brother-in-law know what had been going on. Sidney took a deep breath before knocking on the door. After greeting her family for a few minutes she recounted the story for what seemed like the hundredth time and prepared herself for the storm that Sidra was about to unleash.

But her sister was calm, unusually so. "So all the devil had to do was point a finger and start a rumor...?"

Sidney nodded. "And all the good church people said amen." She paused and then almost as an after-thought said, "Or, at least the ones with no discernment. Apparently I was expecting too much when I anticipated that Christians would pray or use discernment after hearing gossip."

"No you weren't!" The outburst was loud and angry.

She was taken aback because it wasn't Sidra but Jensen who exploded. She stole a glance at her sister who was still. Jensen had started pacing the floor and mumbling to himself. They weren't sure if he was praying or cursing under is breath. Neither sister had ever seen him so agitated.

He stopped pacing to address both women. "Does he have any idea what he's done? How many lives will be affected by his actions?" The disbelief was visibly written on his face. "He probably only had twenty to twenty-five percent of his membership that are actually mature enough to handle this foolishness. The rest of those people may wander around for years not ever trusting another church or preacher again. Some of them are likely to turn away from Christianity altogether and all because of this! Thousands and thousands of souls hanging in the balance and he just decides to throw them all away to get you out of his system!" He paced for several more minutes before he grabbed his coat and car keys. He swallowed Sidney up in a hug then brushed his lips across Sidra's before pulling back to look in her eyes. "Baby, I'm sorry but I have got to get out of here."

Sidra touched his face tenderly and nodded with understanding. "I know. Tell Pastor Williams I said hello."

He was gone in a flash leaving the two sisters staring at each other in silence.

Sidra was the first to speak. "Umm, Sidney I think you should know that..."

"Jensen's been called into the ministry."

"How did you..?"

"The apostolic ministry to be exact." At her sister's questioning look she simply shrugged her shoulders. "It's all over him. He's wearing it like a cloak."

Sidra's eyes began to fill with tears as she pulled her sister into a hug. "Thank you God for the confirmation we asked for and for blessing my sister with Your gifts."

There is nothing covered that will not be revealed, nor hidden that will not be known ~ Jesus

CHAPTER 12

The headline of the newspaper the next morning read *Leaving Canaan.* The article went on to explain chapter and verse of Canaan's plan for Sidney as related by an undisclosed source in law enforcement. Every sordid detail and person involved was laid bare for everyone who picked up a newspaper that morning. They also disclosed that the church's board had decided to remove Canaan from the pastorate while they reviewed the details of the case. They did this to try to stem the mass exodus of their congregation.

It seems that every member of the church, anyone who ever visited the church and anyone who had ever flipped past the church's religious broadcast on the TV bought a newspaper that morning. Indeed, the company had to do a second printing before the evening was out.

No one could get enough of the wayward pastor and his dysfunctional family. The media's frenzied feeding lasted well over a month. Knowing the madness that would ensue, Sidney had given her statement to the police and left town before the first edition rolled off the presses. She went to visit her Uncle Ward for a couple of weeks but stayed in constant contact with Sidra for updates on the case or in case she was ever needed to testify. When she came back, she stayed out of the public eye as long as she could.

The FBI had handed over all their surveillance data over to the appropriate local authorities. Because of this, Canaan and his sons were each looking at spending several years in a federal prison. Damaris was also charged with cyber-stalking and sentenced to some jail time.

The man that handed over the equipment in the first place received a slap on the wrist but because he was the one who brought the situation to light, received no jail time. That technology that they used so freely was the nail in their coffin. They might not have even been caught except for the fact that it was used too often. They were tracked by the frequency of the signals they were using to track Sidney. Ensnared by their own trap and facing plenty of years behind bars, Canaan and his sons sang like canaries by turning on everyone involved. Every postal worker that held her mail, every phone company employee who blocked a call and every person at the church who had even the smallest part to play was spotlighted. Rev. Fitzhugh's name came up more than once as Canaan spilled his guts. All of the people lost their jobs. Most lost much more than that.

By the time Justice read the complete file all he could do was shake his head and then shake it again. It turns out that there were several pastors across the country that had been keeping very close tabs on specific members. Of the cases the FBI knew about, Sidney was one of twelve. The information about the other churches, offered up freely by the right Reverend Fitzhugh in exchange for no jail time, proved to be invaluable. The media was not made aware of the other churches. The agents involved hoped that this would give them time to study the pastors and people involved.

Several agents, Justice and Terrence included, were assigned to the new cases. The plan was to hopefully be able to do the same thing in those cases that they had done for Sidney. Justice didn't like it. Canaan Styles had just proven what he'd already known for a lifetime. Most church leaders were out for themselves. Where Terrence was immersed in his new faith and ecstatic with his new assignment, Justice couldn't have cared less. He spent two weeks back in D.C. with his family and friends before flying out for the new assignment.

***

Terrence walked into Jensen's home office behind Justice and he was slightly agitated. He closed the door after Justice sat down behind the desk but he couldn't sit still though, not yet. He paced back and forth for a while unable to settle his mind. Justice leaned back in his chair and watched his friend. He knew better than to say anything before Terrence was ready. Justice picked up his coffee mug sitting on the warmer and waited for several minutes for his friend to calm down. They had been in plenty of life and death situations together before so he had seen Terrence in action but just like now he knew this was his friends' way of dealing with tense situations. He paced back and forth until his mind had broken everything down to the most basic of levels.

Several minutes later, Terrence took a seat across from Justice and just stared at him.

"She's a sensitive."

Justice didn't flinch. They had both been at the agency long enough to see some things that could not be explained, no matter how hard one tried. If this job had taught him nothing else, it showed him that there were much deeper and wiser things than he roaming the planet they all called home. He would even go so far as to admit that they weren't alone. He wasn't ready to sign up on the UFO bandwagon just yet but he knew too much, had seen too many unexplainable occurrences at this point in his life to write them off as coincidence. The best they could do was slap a label on it and keep it moving. He looked at his friend to make sure nothing else was coming. "So, Sidney is psychic?"

"Yes. No. She calls it prophetic. It was a gift God gave her after she got 'saved'."

"So what's the difference between psychic and prophetic?" Justice leaned forward placing his mug back on the warmer and waited on the answer.

"Sidney says she knows where her stuff is coming from. Her information is coming from God."

"And you believe her?"

Terrence leaned back in the chair and looked at the man he had grown close to over the years. "I know I saw some stuff last week that I can't explain. I know there are things walking around out there we know nothing about. I also know I was about ready to drop this job to find out what I don't know."

"You're serious?"

"Yeah," He grinned. "But then I decided I could get educated and keep a paycheck all at the same time. This new assignment is just icing."

"OK, so where are you going to get educated?"

"Your sister-in-law's old church."

Justice's left eyebrow went up into a full arch and Terrence grinned. "Sidra's not Sidney's"

"Oh. You had me worried for minute."

Terrence shook his head. "No worries there. I don't need to see Canaan Styles for a long time."

Justice nodded. "That's a good thing because he'll be locked up for a long time."

Terrence stood up to move the chair he was sitting in closer to the desk. "I'll tell you one thing though, If Sidney is free when I get back from Chicago, I'm coming straight back to D.C. and I'm going to put a rock on her left hand."

"Man, your assignment there is only for three or four months, tops."

"Exactly."

Justice laughed but he knew the other man was as serious as a heart attack. "I wouldn't go ring shopping just yet."

Terrence stopped mid-step. "Why not?"

"You know the actor that shadows me for that TV crime drama?"

"The super star, yeah what about him?"

"He's been asking to meet Sidney and he's been into all that God stuff for a while, like her." Justice held both hands in front of him to offer his friend a 'better luck next time' gesture.

"Humph." Terrence reached the door and opened it. "He's got three, four months tops and then I'm going to crash his party."

Justice waited for the office door to close before he picked up the phone. He had seen that look on Terrence's face before and it prompted him to make the call sooner rather than later. "Hey man, it's Justice. My family is having a cookout in

D.C. next weekend and I wanted to know if you wanted to join us?" He let the other man speak and then nodded. "Yes, Sidney will be there. Alright good, I'll get back to you with the date and times and all that."

***

"Sidney, I really am sorry for all the trouble I caused you. I'm sorry for everything."

She took Walker's hand as they walked toward the door. "Walker, please it's fine. I mean it turned out that way anyway. I'm still alive. No harm done."

"Yeah no thanks to me, I'm surprised they even let me keep my job, even with the demotion."

"You shouldn't be. It was because of your and my aunt's testimonies, that they searched Winston's desk and home and found the pictures Adam doctored of me several years ago along with records connecting him to Styles. You made a mistake but you did what you could to correct it. They're going to review your file in a few months to see if you can be moved back to your regular position right?"

"Yes, I just feel so bad."

"Don't and don't beat yourself up over it. Believe it or not that was part of the process I had to go through to get to where I needed to be."

"What do you mean?"

"Think about the stories of Joseph and David and even Jesus in the bible."

"Yeah?"

"Some kind of way God takes rejection and betrayal, especially by those closest to you, and uses it to build you up, make you stronger and take you to the next level."

"I never thought about it like that."

Sidney gave a half smile. "Trust me, I didn't either. At least not in this fashion, until I found myself in the middle of it."

"So God uses it all huh?" Walker was amazed at her calmness with everything going on around her.

"Yeah, that little revelation came after the fact. I hope the others got it too. How many did you say there were? I mean of us who were being..."

"Stalked is a good word for it."

Sidney gave a rueful glance. "Okay then stalked."

"Looks like an even dozen. We're still trying to go through Pas... I mean Styles' records along with the other pastor's files but we believe it was only twelve of you."

"Wow, well I hope and pray the other eleven get the same revelation when it's time."

"I'm praying the same thing. If what we found in your case was normal operating procedure, God help us all."

"What do you mean?" She had left town so quickly, she missed most of the reported details about what was found.

"Oh, that's right, you didn't hear most of it. Well for starters, we found your forks under the bed of the pastor's youngest child."

"What?"

"Yeah, for the record, something's just not right about that kid. Anyway, both boys and your friend Damaris would go through your house when you were gone and take whatever they wanted. Damaris took most of the Jewelry but Mrs. Styles received some of it as a present from her youngest son. Everything you reported missing was found except oddly enough one charm."

"Which one?"

"You had a little globe."

"Oh yeah, I use to wear it on a chain around my neck."

He nodded. "Right, I remember. Well, that's the only thing we didn't find. Also, we discovered what they were doing when they were accessing your social networking accounts."

"I don't know if I want to hear this."

"Just say the word and I will keep my trap sealed."

She thought about it only for a moment. "No, not knowing is going to drive me crazy sooner or later. You may as well tell me now."

"OK, well you were right about them driving all the religious people away on Twitter but they were also sending out information that would attract those most church people would deem outright sinners."

Sidney laughed at that term. "As opposed to the under cover sinners that they were."

"Exactly. In fact it was your online friendships with those non-church people that they used to drive the church people away."

She smiled again. "That's OK. They probably did me a favor. Church people who are afraid of sinners would have had a problem with me sooner or later. It's all right though, they did the same thing to Jesus."

He smiled as he acknowledged the truth in her statement. "I guess they did. And as far as Facebook, we've determined that most of the 'friends' that they deleted happened to be people that they couldn't influence but still had some clout or connections."

"So, in other words, anyone who may have actually been able to do something about this foolishness, was deleted?"

"Yes, and don't get me started on Dirk."

She made a face when she heard the name. "Something about him just makes my skin crawl."

"I can see that. I'm hoping to God that he gets straightened out in prison. Lord only knows the harm that was done when Styles called that boy into the ministry. His mind couldn't handle what he perceived as that much power. He went absolutely crazy. Some of the stuff he did..."

"Yeah, I definitely don't want to know that."

"No, you really don't. Let's just say he gave the term 'drunk with power' a whole new meaning."

Sidney was saddened at the loss of potential. *If only he had met the right Christians.* "God help him."

The world is round and the place which may seem like the end may also be only the beginning. ~ Ivy Baker

Epilogue

****

Several months later...

The phone rang just as Sidney was settling into bed.

"Hello?"

"Sidney? I am so sorry to be calling you at this hour. I know it must be night time on your side of the world but it is an emergency." The thickly accented voice sounded heavy with concern.

"There's no problem Excellency. I hadn't fallen asleep yet."

"Good. I would like for you to come this weekend if possible. I've been having the same dream for three nights in a row. There is much to discuss. We have already made provision for you and your actor friend if he would like to come as well."

"Thank you, Emir. That was very kind of you. I'm not sure about his schedule but I will see you this weekend."

"Outstanding!"

"And Excellency?"

"Yes, my dear. What is it?"

"You really don't have to stack all those gifts in my room this time. I felt slightly uncomfortable the last time I was there. I mean... there was so much."

The amused ruler laughed at her humility. "My dear girl, that is the way things are done around here for someone like you. You may as well get used to it. How do they say in your country? This is... how we roll." His laughter could be heard echoing throughout the room.

Sidney returned the laughter and shook her head. "Thank you Excellency. I will see you soon." She hung up the phone and looked over at the handsome man lying beside her. He propped himself up on one elbow and waited for her to speak. There was a mischievous glint in her eyes when she turned to him and said "Are you busy this weekend or would you like to spend some time in Dubai?"

He reached up and grabbed a handful of hair to pull her down for the kiss he'd been waiting patiently to give her. "Like I'm going to let my wife go to Dubai alone. I saw the way those men over there looked at you, just like that agent...what's his name?"

Sidney looked innocent and her eyes grew big. "Who Terrence?"

"Who, Terrence?" He had raised his voice 5 octaves in an attempt to mimic hers and he still missed the mark. "Don't play innocent with me. I know full well that if I hadn't pulled a ring out that night, he would have."

She smiled as she snuggled closer to him. "Yeah you're probably right." When they had settled down, she turned to him and rubbed the five o'clock shadow that had grown under his chin over the weekend. "And we should probably let everyone know we're married now."

He nuzzled her neck while she tried to pull away from the scratchy sensation. "Mmhmm. I hope you don't mind but I told my publicist to release the news on Monday morning. And now that we're going to Dubai we may as well make a real honeymoon of it."

Sidney looked up in awe at the handsome face. *God really does give you double for your trouble.* "Sounds like a plan to me. No reporters, no paparazzi..."

"No one around to disturb us..."

She sat back up quickly and turned to face him. "I promise this is the last time I'll ask, but you are OK with an instant family right? I mean, adopting Maya and having her come live with us works for you right?"

He sat up next to her and pulled her closer. "For the last time, you two are what I prayed for. I told you I'd spent the better part of my life pursuing my career and that left little time for a real personal life?"

"Yes."

"What I didn't tell you is that when I got saved, my options for a wife were drastically reduced, especially in the field of acting and especially in L.A. I was seriously beginning to think that I was going to die a single man. I was looking around at all my friends and their families and honestly thought I would never get to experience that. An instant family is ...well it's more than I thought God would bless me with. I love you and Maya and Alex and even Meena."

Sidney giggled when she thought about her aunt and the new changes she was dealing with.

He laughed with her. "You know, I think she's warming up to me."

"Yeah, you're probably right." She laughed again. Since Meena had become 'more human' (as Alex put it) in recent months, Aunt Alex agreed to let her move in with her. Initially, Alex said it was because the place would be too quiet without Maya but Sidney knew, God had touched the hearts of both her aunts and restored her family. She felt only a tinge of sadness when she thought about her mother and wished Olivia were alive to see her sisters together now.

"Hey, I don't like it when you get too quiet. What are you thinking about?"

Sidney grinned at her new love. "Just thinking about life and God and how you never really know what you're going to get when you mix them together."

"No you don't, but you can be sure, when everything is said and done, it will be good."

Sidney smiled. "Real good!"

*   *   *   *

Return to the stronghold, you prisoners of hope. Even today I declare that I will restore double to you ~ God

(Zechariah 9:12)

END

Dear Readers,

I hope you enjoyed Sidney's story. I plan to follow this book with other books focusing on different characters previously introduced in the series. If you'd like to read more stories like this one, please contact me and let me know which characters you'd like to hear more about. You can contact me via a social network, email me or go to my website and leave a note in my guestbook on the last page. I've included the information below.

I want to thank my friends who were very encouraging during my sophomore project. Thank you Darling, Ms. Bessie and Aunt Janice for going above and beyond with your promotion and support. Thank you LaVerne for your suggestion about an upcoming book. I wasn't thinking about that character but I heard you and I'll get on it. ;-)

While I'm thinking about it, I want to mention a book I read while I was writing this one. The author is Dutch Sheets and the book is entitled "Authority In Prayer". That book and a message by Joel Osteen entitled "Mountain Moving Faith" were very instrumental in helping me complete this book. Also, if anyone is interested in learning more about spiritual gifts, there is a book by Lester Sumrall titled The Gifts and Ministries of The Holy Spirit that gives a great breakdown of God given gifts.

Finally, a BIG shout-out goes to everyone who took the time to leave a review or comment or rating on Barnes&Noble, Amazon and/or my website. You'll never know how much I'm encouraged by those remarks. To anyone I may have forgotten, thank you. I appreciate all of you.

I would love to hear from you. My contact info is below.

Email: amckayauthor@aol.com

Website: www.audreymckay.net

Facebook: Enough Good News by Audrey McKay

Twitter :   @DreyMcK

I pray God's richest blessings for your life
Audrey